49

The Challenge

Carter extended his arms away from his body, inviting a search. If the big man was wary, he didn't show it. He approached Carter and patted him down. As he was bent over, Carter suddenly clenched both hands together, making one large fist, and brought them down on the base of the man's neck.

The big man staggered and went down on one knee. Carter stepped back as the troops surrounding him raised their weapons, the noise audible even at a distance.

"Merde," the big man swore in French. He got heavily to his feet, looked into Carter's eyes for a few long seconds, and then without warning doubled his fist and smashed it into Carter's chest, knocking him backward, taking his breath away.

Carter pulled himself together and straightened up. He smiled. "One-on-one, scum," he said softly in gutter French. "Just you and me."

Surprise flickered in the man's eyes. He nodded. "That would give me a great deal of pleasure, monsieur . . . "

NICK CARTER IS IT!

FROM THE NICK CARTER
KILLMASTER SERIES

DRAGONFIRE

KILL MASTER

NICK CARTER

JOVE BOOKS, NEW YORK

"Nick Carter" is a registered trademark of The Condé Nast Publications, Inc., registered in the United States Patent Office.

KILLMASTER #234: DRAGONFIRE

A Jove book / published by arrangement with
The Condé Nast Publications, Inc.

PRINTING HISTORY
Jove edition / February 1988

ISBN: 0-515-09444-7

Jove Books are published by The Berkley Publishing Group,
200 Madison Avenue, New York, New York 10016.
The name "JOVE" and the "J" logo
are trademarks belonging to Jove Publications, Inc.

PRINTED IN THE UNITED STATES OF AMERICA

10 9 8 7 6 5 4 3 2 1

*Dedicated to the men of the
Secret Services of the
United States of America*

PROLOGUE

A thick, blue-gray mist hung over the slowly moving Chao Phraya River in central Bangkok as the tall, distinguished-looking American left the Metropolitan Police headquarters and got into a waiting Mercedes sedan. The hour was nearly midnight, and Gordon Guthrie, number one man for Central Intelligence Agency activities in Thailand, was in a foul mood. At fifty he was nearing the age where he would be pulled out of the field and brought back to Langley to man a foreign desk. In his case, the Southeast Asia spot would be his for asking. He'd been bouncing around the region for the past twenty years and had become, by reason of longevity, and a bit of intelligence, an expert. "The inscrutable Oriental mind is a myth," he was fond of saying. "Once you acknowledge their value system—that rice and fish are more important than either democracy or communism—their way of thinking becomes quite comprehensible."

That evening he was deeply disturbed. A lot of recent work seemed on the verge of going down the drain, and he said as much to his number two man, who was seated in the back of the Mercedes.

"Colonel Trat told me point-blank that his hands were

1

tied. There wasn't a damned thing he could—or would—do for us.''

Carlton Reed, assistant chief of the Bangkok station, shook his head. ''It was about what we expected, Gordon. Kangting is a powerful man. It's pretty tough going up against him.''

''And it'll be a damned sight tougher once he goes over to the Chinese,'' Guthrie added ruefully. ''But the whole business is outside Trat's province. It's a matter for the politicians; for the government, not for some colonel in the Metropolitan Police.''

Their driver, a Thai national, pulled out smoothly into the still thick Friday night traffic and headed back toward the American embassy across town on Wireless Road.

Guthrie sank back in his seat and tried to think it out. He'd done everything by the book, and yet now was powerless. Six months earlier one of his field men had reported seeing someone who looked very much like Robert Kangting, possibly the richest man in all of Southeast Asia, in the tiny town of Nong Khai, right on the border with Laos and very near the capital city of Vientiane. The CIA had gone up there because it was suspected that Chinese agents were using Laos, and especially the capital city, as a corridor down into Thailand. The rumors—and there were always rumors in Asia—didn't mean much in themselves; the Chinese were always infiltrating one country or another. But this time the rumors seemed to be very persistent, very widespread, and held just a hint of something ominous on the horizon.

It was very possible, Guthrie thought, that the Chinese could be getting ready to take over Burma, Laos, and Thailand in the very near future. The fact that Kangting, a billionaire with supposedly strong and friendly ties with the West, had been so close to such activities didn't sit well with Guthrie.

''If Kangting sides with the Chinese, all of Southeast Asia would soon fall out of sheer economic necessity,'' he'd explained in his report to Langley.

"Send us proof," was the terse reply.

Without the help of the Thai police, who were afraid of Kangting's power, proof might be difficult to come by. And Guthrie wanted to avoid using U.S. intelligence operatives. The debacle of Vietnam wasn't that far in the past; the scars remained. Don't upset the apple cart; that had been the order of the day from the moment he had arrived.

"We could put someone on him," Reed suggested. "Twenty-four-hour-a-day coverage. Smother the son of a bitch."

"If our people were made, all hell would break loose," Guthrie said absently, his thoughts elsewhere.

"If he's innocent, we could call it protection."

"His own government might be able to get away with it, not us."

"Then what?" Reed asked.

Guthrie glanced at his colleague. The man was young for the job, but in less than seven years with the Company, he had built an impressive track record, most of it in Eastern Europe. Asia was new to him. And he was impatient.

"The question is, Carlton, why?" Gutherie said softly. "Why would one of the richest men in the world want to deal with the People's Republic? What could the Red Chinese possibly offer him that he doesn't already have?"

"It's certainly not money," Reed agreed.

"Perhaps it's nothing."

"Huh?"

"Perhaps it's a setup. Perhaps it wasn't Kangting our man spotted up north. Perhaps someone is doing a number on us."

"Why?"

"To see what we might do. To gauge our reactions. Test our effectiveness. See just how close our relationship is with the Thai government. Worth a few risks, I'd think."

"It's possible," Reed said after a moment of thought. "Either way, it's something we should know about."

"I agree," Guthrie said. He sat forward. "Chuan?"

"Yes, Mr. Guthrie?" their driver said, glancing in the rearview mirror.

"Let's take a run past Mr. Kangting's compound. Let's see what he's up to this evening."

"Sure thing," Chuan said. He waited for a break in the traffic, then shot behind a *samlor*, one of the motorized three-wheeled taxis that buzzed around Bangkok, and hurried up past the Siam Intercontinental toward the Victory Monument and the highway that led out to the Don Muang Airport.

"He's home," Reed said. "Or at least he was as of eighteen hundred hours."

"Was he alone?"

"The usual entourage."

"You've been watching him?"

Reed grinned. "I just happened to be in the neighborhood, Gordon, when he was coming in from the airport. I didn't hang around very long. I wanted to wait and see what you and Colonel Trat came up with tonight."

Guthrie nodded, and then once again sat back in his seat. He had a bad feeling about all of this. There was something— some fact or some notion—that he was forgetting. Something just around the corner, something that would put everything into perspective for him. Yet for the life of him he couldn't imagine what it might be. He was still working on the answer to the single, simple question: What could the Chinese do or get for Robert Kangting that the billionaire couldn't do or get for himself? It simply didn't make sense.

Robert Kangting held court in a five-acre compound about six miles south of Bangkok's international airport. Besides the main house of fifty rooms, there were quarters for staff, a helipad and hangars, three swimming pools, extensive gardens, and a network of canals that eventually connected with the Chao Phraya. Surrounded by a tall, electrified, barbed-wired-topped fence, and guarded around the clock,

Kangting lived as many billionaires lived—a life quite apart from ordinary people. He traveled extensively aboard his own 747 and on his 280-foot yacht, which was docked in the Gulf of Thailand downriver from Bangkok. Wherever he went he took with him a large retinue of servants, personal staff, women, and bodyguards. It was said that he had a personal army of at least a thousand men, and that it would take federal government troops to arrest him if the need ever arose.

Chuan pulled up in the deep shadows just down the road from the main gate into Kangting's compound and shut off the Mercedes's headlights, though he kept the engine running.

The compound was so brightly lit it could have been daylight inside. Guthrie powered down his window, and immediately they could hear the sounds of music and laughter coming from the compound. Kangting was entertaining tonight, and judging by the noise, it was quite a party.

"Was there anything about this on the wire?" he asked.

"I didn't see a thing," Reed said. Usually when Kangting threw a large party, the wire services knew about it weeks in advance. It was big news.

So why was tonight different? Guthrie wondered. Perhaps because Kangting had invited guests he didn't want to publicize, he speculated.

"It might be interesting to see just who is on the guest list," he said.

Reed grinned. "It might be very interesting at that."

"Stick with the car," Guthrie told their driver, and he and Reed got out and hurried across the road, keeping well away from the lights, until they could duck into the jungle that led back to the fence.

A no-man's-land at least twenty-five feet wide had been cleared on either side of the fence and was lit by strong spotlights raised on stanchions every two hundred feet or so. At the very least Guthrie figured the fence was monitored on close-circuit television, but there were probably armed guards within the compound as well.

He and Reed made their way a few hundred yards back from the road, keeping parallel to the fence but well within the concealing darkness of the jungle. From time to time they would stop and listen to the sounds of the party, which got louder and louder the closer they came to a spot just opposite the main house.

When they had gone far enough, they angled closer to the no-man's-land, the lights from within the compound filtering through the dense underbrush and bamboo.

"Christ . . ." Reed suddenly gasped.

Without warning, the lights along a long stretch of fence went out, and something or someone crashed through the brush to their right. Guthrie stepped back, but as he reached for his gun something very hard and hot slammed into his chest, lifting him off his feet, a great gush of blood, bone, and flesh spewing from a large hole in his back.

The last thing he saw was Reed's skull exploding against the night sky.

ONE

Nick Carter stood on a narrow window ledge just outside the fourth-floor office of the ambassador from Thailand. Forty feet below, two uniformed guards leaned against the hood of a black Cadillac limousine in the brightly lit courtyard. Downtown Washington was a glow in the sky to the south.

The sounds of the party drifted up to him through the open French doors directly below. A group of musicians was playing traditional Thai music, the notes light and delicate on the night air.

Carter wore a perfectly tailored tuxedo, a bit of red silk at his lapel pocket, his patent leather formal pumps gleaming in the night light as he edged closer and put his ear to the window glass.

Robert Kangting had left the party just minutes before with the Thai chargé d'affaires and a Chinese man Carter had not recognized. Together they had come directly upstairs to the ambassador's office. Carter had followed on the stairs, and then had stepped out onto the ledge from a window at the end of the corridor.

"If Kangting goes over to the Communists, so will most

of Southeast Asia,'' David Hawk had told Carter less than twenty-four hours earlier. ''His net worth is estimated at better than three billion dollars.''

It was early evening when Hawk had called Carter and asked him to come to his office at AXE headquarters on Dupont Circle. The week had been quiet, and Carter had planned on heading up to Cape Cod for the weekend with an old friend from Chicago. But when Hawk called he dropped everything.

AXE, fronted by Amalgamated Press and Wire Services, was a small, highly specialized and supersecret intelligence-gathering and special action agency. It was entirely separate from the CIA and the NSA, and worked hard to keep its autonomy and low profile. Hawk was AXE's founder and director, and Carter was his top field man, holding the designation N3: licensed to kill in service to his government.

Hawk had been facing the window of his top-floor office, looking down at the traffic on Massachusetts Avenue, his thick shock of white hair touching his shirt collar, when Carter came in.

''Good evening, sir,'' Carter said.

Hawk turned around, his omnipresent foul cigar clenched firmly between his teeth. His tie was loose and his sleeves were rolled up. He looked as if he hadn't slept in two days. Something was up, but Carter knew better than to press for an opening. Hawk would present the case in his own way.

''I have a job for you, Nick. And it's probably going to turn out to be a nasty one. Lots of opportunities to step on some big toes. Some wrong toes, too, so you're going to have to be very careful.''

Hawk waved to a chair across from his cluttered desk, and when he and Carter were settled, he thumbed slowly through a thick file folder. When he looked up he shook his head, as if he were at a loss where to begin. Carter had rarely seen his boss like that, and it was disturbing. Hawk was an old pro. He had been in the business for a lot of years, first with the OSS, then with the CIA, and eventually the driving force behind AXE.

"Does the name Robert Kangting mean anything to you, Nick?" he finally began.

"A billionaire. The Adnan Kashoghi of Southeast Asia."

"That's close enough. What would you say to the speculation that Kangting might be getting ready to defect to China?"

Carter shrugged. "I'd say whoever was making the speculation had to be wrong. They'd have nothing to offer him. Everything he stands for is exactly the opposite of what the Chinese believe. He'd be stripped of his power, his money. It doesn't make a whole lot of sense."

"No, it certainly doesn't. And yet it just may be true."

"Anyone else in on this, sir?"

"The CIA has been working on it for several months out of their Bangkok station. Apparently Kangting was seen on the northern Thai border at the same time the Chinese were working some sort of infiltration project."

"Was he working with them?"

"They weren't sure. The station chief out there, a guy named Gordon Guthrie, filed his report—which I saw—and Langley told him they needed rock-solid evidence before anything could be done. Kangting is simply too powerful a man for us to take any chances."

"And Guthrie found the proof?"

Again Hawk seemed to hesitate. He took the cigar out of his mouth and looked at the chewed end, then put it down. "Last night Guthrie, his number two man, Carlton Reed, and their Thai driver, Lawrence Chuan, turned up dead outside the town of Lop Buri—that's about seventy-five miles north of Bangkok. They'd been shot to death."

"What were they doing up there?"

"Probably nothing," Hawk said. "It's more likely they were murdered in Bangkok, and then their bodies were dumped. The Thai police are convinced they were murdered by bandits. They were robbed, and their bodies were mutilated."

"But you don't think so."

"No," Hawk said heavily. "Guthrie apparently went to see a Thai cop, Colonel Phuket Trat, about Kangting that night. A few hours later he turned up dead. That's too much of a coincidence for me—and for the Company. They've asked for our help on this one. The Bangkok station is in a shambles, and if it was Kangting's people, they'll be watching the Agency very closely."

"When do I leave, sir?" Carter asked. He knew Bangkok well, though it had been a number of years since he'd been there last. He still had a few friends bouncing around the area, friends who owed him a favor or two.

"You don't have to go anywhere at the moment. Kangting is due in Washington in the morning. There's to be some sort of a reception for him at the Thai embassy up on Kalorama Road. The Secretary of State will be there, along with a half-dozen senators. Your invitation is here." Hawk handed across a thick packet of material. "I've included Kangting's background, along with Guthrie's and Reed's files."

"What's my cover?"

"You'll be a naval commander. Military liaison with the Thai government. A new assignment. You don't officially assume your duties until the end of the month. We're just introducing you around for the moment. It'll give you freedom to move between Washington and Thailand if the need arises."

"What if I find nothing? Maybe Guthrie was on a wild-goose chase."

"Then you find nothing, Nick," Hawk said, leaning forward. "But Guthrie and the other two were not killed by bandits—I'd bet almost anything on it—which means that whoever did do it will be watching for someone else, someone like you, to show up."

"Might it be the Chinese themselves, using Kangting as bait?"

"The thought has occurred to us. So you're going to have

to watch your step. And that means with the Thai police as well. You won't be able to trust anyone out there. But it is absolutely essential that we know one way or another: Is Kangting going over to the Chinese or isn't he? The fate of all of Southeast Asia depends on it. The entire region could become another Vietnam.''

The curtains on the ambassador's window were closed, the sounds from within the room muffled. Carter could hear someone talking, but he couldn't quite make out the words, though he could tell they were speaking Thai or perhaps even Chinese—one of the major languages in Thailand—because of the singsong tones.

He crouched down and tried the window. It was unlocked. He slid it open half an inch.

''An ambitious plan,'' Carter heard Kangting say in Thai. It was a language the Killmaster had only a fair knowledge of, though he understood enough to catch the gist of a conversation.

''But you are an ambitious man,'' said the chargé d'affaires.

''Ten years is a long time to wait, and I am getting no younger,'' Kangting said.

''But there is much profit to be made in the anticipation, you understand,'' suggested the Chinese man.

Kangting laughed.

''Nor are you so old, sir, that you would not be able to appreciate the outcome. It would be well worth your while. Well worth it.''

Again Kangting laughed. ''Already there are questions . . .''

''Which we will take care of for you. You have my assurances,'' the Chinese gentleman said.

''And mine,'' the chargé added.

''Wars have been fought for less,'' Kangting said. The curtains stirred. He was at the window.

Carter straightened his tall, well-built body and stepped

aside just as the curtains were pulled back, light from inside the room spilling out into the night.

"And won," the Chinese man said strongly.

Carter flattened against the wall. Kangting's guards below had noticed the light and were looking up. Carter held his breath. They'd have to spot him. Even though he was in the shadows, his formal shirt was white and would have to stand out.

"Is the prize worth the risk?" Kangting asked. He was less than two feet from Carter.

"Only you can answer that," the chargé said.

"Yes," Kangting agreed. The curtains fell back.

The guards below in the courtyard were still looking up. One turned away, but the other one was looking directly at Carter. He stepped a few feet to the left, said something to the other man, and pointed directly up at the Killmaster.

They'd made him, or they were about to. It was essential, however, that no one see his face. If that happened, his effectiveness in Thailand once he arrived would drop to zero.

He turned quickly, so that he was facing the wall, and started along the ledge toward the far corner of the building.

"Hey!" one of the guards below shouted in alarm. "Hey, you!"

Carter kept moving.

Someone else shouted something, and a moment later a half-dozen men rushed out into the courtyard, the sounds of their footfalls sharp on the cobblestones below. A truck started up, headlights came on, and it swung around sharply from the front gate. A moment later the bright beam of a spotlight flashed just behind Carter.

He stopped, pulled his 9mm Luger from the holster beneath his left armpit, and fired a shot over his shoulder just as the spotlight centered on him. The light went out. But he had run out of time.

Carter was three feet from the next window. He reached it just as the first shot from a silenced pistol ricocheted off the wall inches from his head. The curtains were open and the room within was dark. He tried the window, which was unlocked. He shoved it open and dived inside just as another spotlight came into life, flashing against the side of the building.

He lay there in the darkness on the floor for a long moment, listening to the sounds of shouting and seeing the flashes of the spotlight outside. They knew he had been on the ledge and now he was gone. But they did not know for certain which window he had entered.

The light came on and Carter rolled over, bringing his Luger up, his finger pressing on the trigger. A young woman in her mid-twenties, her long black hair pinned up and crowned with a diamond tiara, stared at him with dark eyes as she stood in the doorway to a luxurious bathroom. She was dressed in a strapless evening gown, her shoulders tiny and delicate, her breasts rising and falling as she breathed. Her mouth was open in surprise, but she made no sound.

Carter pointed the Luger away from her and got to his feet, avoiding the window. "Pardon me," he said.

The young woman's eyes flicked from the window to the Luger in Carter's hand and back again. "Do you always enter a woman's bedroom in this fashion?" she asked once she'd regained her composure. She spoke English with a lilting Thai accent.

Carter lowered his gun. "Someone out there doesn't like me."

She smiled. "Are you a spy?"

"No. But the Chinese think so."

"Ah," she said. "The Chinese."

There was a commotion in the corridor. Carter stepped aside so that he would not be in a direct line with the doorway when they came through. "I think you'd better get back into the bathroom. Just for a moment," Carter said softly, in Thai.

The woman's eyes opened wide. She glanced at the door. Someone pounded on it.

"Inside!" she hissed. "I'll take care of them."

Carter hesitated only a moment, then crossed the room and stepped into the huge bathroom. The young woman looked up into his eyes, then closed the door. Her cheeks were flushed and her breathing rapid.

"Yes! It's about time!" she yelled.

Carter could hear the door to her suite open.

"Elizabeth, are you all right?" It was Kangting.

"Of course I am, no thanks to them," she snapped.

"Is he here?" someone else asked.

"No, you idiot," the woman replied angrily. "Whoever he was, he burst through the window, shoved me down, and went out the door. What sort of security is this?"

"I'm so very sorry, miss."

"Well, don't just stand there! Get him! I don't particularly appreciate being knocked down in my own bedroom!"

"Of course . . ."

The room was quiet for a moment. "Are you sure you're all right?" Kangting asked again.

"Perfectly."

"I'll join you in a few minutes," Kangting said.

"I was just leaving," she told him.

The door closed, and the room fell silent. Carter waited for a minute or two, the sounds of the search fading in the corridor and outside in the courtyard, before he opened the door a crack and looked out into the bedroom. They'd all gone.

He stepped out of the bathroom, crossed the room to the corridor door, and opened it just enough so that he could look out. Two men in dark business suits stood near the elevator. They were deep in discussion, one of them poking his finger in the other's chest. The elevator arrived, they got on, closed the iron gate, and the car descended.

When they were out of sight, Carter holstered his Luger, slipped out of the room, and hurried the opposite way to the far end of the corridor and into the stairwell. Someone was below, footsteps echoing up to him. He listened for a moment or two, but the sounds faded. Whoever it was had gone downstairs.

He started down himself, hesitating at the first landing, listening, every sense straining to detect someone else below. But there was nothing. The search was apparently concentrated elsewhere, probably up on the roof.

The third-floor corridor was deserted, but the second-floor corridor was packed with guests in formal attire. The stairwell and elevator faced each other from opposite ends of the building. A formal staircase rising from the grand hall below split the corridor in two. No one seemed to be aware that anything unusual had happened, or that a search of the building and the grounds was being conducted. Evidently the general hubbub had been loud enough to cover the sound of his unsilenced single shot.

Carter waited for a moment until no one appeared to be looking his way, then he slipped out into the corridor and moved smoothly away from the stairwell door, snagging a glass of champagne from a passing waiter.

The corridor opened onto a broad balcony that overlooked the grand hall below. A bar had been set up to the right of the stairs, a long buffet table to the left. A lot of people were congregated around both. Carter recognized a number of the Americans, and a few people from some of the other embassies. Washington was a party town. Ordinarily there would not have been a lot of big shots at the Thai embassy, but tonight Robert Kangting was present, and money always drew power.

Carter eased toward the balcony rail just as the elevator opened downstairs and the women Kangting had called Elizabeth stepped out. Immediately she was surrounded and someone brought her a drink. They all moved off in a group, her laughter drifting up to him over the music.

He finished his champagne, lit a cigarette, and moved across to the bar where he ordered a scotch. When he had his drink he meandered downstairs. Elizabeth was across the room in front of the musicians, who had just finished playing something, and their leader was speaking intently to a thick-shouldered man.

Carter crossed the great room directly to where the young woman stood. She looked up at the last moment and spotted him, her eyes widening just a bit. But then she smiled, and came forward.

"Ah, there you are," she said. "I wondered where you had gotten yourself off to."

"Hello, Elizabeth," Carter said.

She came to him and kissed his cheek. "What's your name?" she whispered.

"Nick Carson. Commander Carson. Naval liaison."

She stepped back, still smiling. "I thought you'd have been gone by now," she said, her lips hardly moving.

Carter shrugged. "We hadn't been formally introduced."

She started to laugh, but suddenly cut it off, spotting someone behind Carter.

Carter turned as Robert Kangting and the Thai chargé d'affaires came across the room. The musicians started to play the Thai national anthem, and the room began to applaud.

Kangting brushed past Carter and took Elizabeth into his arms and kissed her lightly on the cheek. "Have you been behaving yourself?" he asked.

"Of course not, Father," she said. "I wouldn't want to disappoint you."

The Thai chargé laughed nervously. He bowed as Elizabeth turned to him. "Good evening, Mr. Phay."

"Good evening, Miss Kangting."

"Father, let me present Commander Nick Carson, naval liaison. We've been having a most interesting conversation."

Kangting bowed slightly, his shrewd eyes narrowing as he surveyed and catalogued Carter. "I thought Lieutenant Commander Wilson held that post, Commander Carson."

"Yes, sir. I don't actually take over until next month."

The Thai chargé was watching Carter with unconcealed interest. If he checked with the Pentagon or with State, he'd find that a Commander Carson was indeed assigned to become the new naval liaison next month. Hawk never did anything by halves, especially when it concerned his premier agent.

"Will you be coming to Bangkok soon?"

"I would suspect so, sir. Perhaps in the next few days."

"Excellent", Kangting said. "When you arrive you most certainly must join us for dinner. "He glanced at his daughter and smiled slightly. "I would like to find out just what sort of interesting conversations you have been having with my daughter."

Kangting's tone was pleasant, but the threat was unmistakable, as was the message: Hands off.

Carter left the reception early and returned to his brownstone in Georgetown. He took a quick shower, poured himself a brandy, put on a jazz tape, and read through the files Hawk had given him. His plane for San Francisco left first thing in the morning; his connecting flight to Bangkok would leave later that afternoon.

The available information on Kangting was sketchy at best, with a lot of speculation in place of hard fact. "So goes Kangting's fortune, so goes the fortunes of Thailand," one of the compilers had written.

Kangting had control, according to the report, over much of the commerce of Thailand, Malaya, Borneo, Sumatia, Java . . . in fact over most of Indonesia. He was constantly on the move—Bangkok, Rangoon, Hong Kong, Berlin, Paris, and lately even Washington, D.C.

He was born in Burma in the late 1920s of a white missionary father and a Chinese mother. His parents were killed by the Japanese and he barely managed to escape to Hong Kong, where the teenager changed his name and hid himself.

After the war he built a fortune in black market food and cigarettes, and at first mostly stolen penicillin. Later he expanded his operation to include opium and cocaine. It was only in the last twenty years that he'd moved legitimately into banking, shipping, radio, and newspapers. He built the first shopping centers in the Far East, and still held a big edge on his competition. Whatever he touched turned to gold.

But he was a private man, in so far as one so wealthy can be private. Wherever he traveled he took with him his personal security force, supposedly the best money could buy. Carter suspected the guards in the compound who had fired the shots up at him had to have been Thai embassy personnel and not Kangting's people: he didn't think the latter would have missed.

When Carter was finished, he packed a single leather bag, and then secured his weapons in his specially designed cassette tape player/radio with a pop-out circuit board. First in was his Luger, along with a silencer and extra clips of 9mm ammunition. The weapon was well oiled and well used. Every so often the AXE armorer suggested he adopt a more modern gun, but Carter always refused. Wilhelmina had saved his life on too many occasions. It was an old friend, as was Hugo, a razor-sharp stiletto that he wore strapped to his right forearm in a chamois sheath. Finally he packed Pierre, a tiny, egg-shaped gas bomb, small but deadly.

Before he secured the circuit board over his weapons he found himself thinking for a moment about the deaths this trio had caused. And about how that number would continue to grow . . . . undoubtedly.

TWO

The full force of a Southeast Asian June evening closed in on Nick Carter the instant he stepped from the 747 at Bangkok's Don Muang Airport. Even before he had retrieved his luggage, his shirt and jacket were plastered to his back. A thousand unfamiliar odors mingled not unpleasantly in a thick mist that seemed to rise over the city of four million people every evening.

Nothing seemed to have changed since the last time he had been in Thailand. The people seemed to do everything in a babble of conversation with a cheerful inefficiency. Bangkok was a city in which the twentieth century had never quite gained a firm foothold. Even the most modern hotels and buildings had a Victorian ambience that was charming.

He was passed through customs with a minimum of fuss and only a perfunctory check of his luggage. Just past the barrier he was met on the busy main floor by Ian Pharr, the CIA's number three man who was, for the moment at least, in charge of the Bangkok station. He'd been told that an experienced agent was coming to look into the murder of Guthrie and Reed, but Carter's specific governmental affiliation was left purposefully vague.

"Welcome to Thailand. Pleasant flight?"

"I could use a shower and a stiff drink," Carter said.

19

Pharr was a slightly built, pleasant-looking young man in his late twenties who had been with the Company barely five years. His mother was Oriental, his father British, still working for the SIS in London after serving many years in Southeast Asia. The younger Pharr had become a naturalized U.S. citizen after serving in the air force and had come to the Company with high marks. So far, according to what Carter had read about him, he'd disappointed no one.

"I can manage the stiff drink in short order," Pharr said as they started across to the main entrance. "But your shower, I'm afraid, is going to have to wait for just a bit."

"Trouble?" Carter asked.

"Nuisance is more like it. Just how in-depth was your briefing concerning the local politics?"

"Not very."

"Well, the number one man as far as law enforcement goes in Bangkok is a character by the name of Phuket Trat."

"Colonel Trat. Guthrie went to see him the night he was killed."

"Right. He answers directly to the Minister of the Interior, not the mayor. Trat thinks he owns the city. But when it comes to any sort of a real crunch, the man falls apart."

"Communist?"

Pharr looked at Carter with new respect, but shrugged. "Who knows? The point is, he knows we're conducting our own investigation, and he talked to the American ambassador yesterday. He told him point-blank that he would personally brief each and every investigator the moment he stepped off the plane. And he meant the *moment*. You're not even supposed to go to your hotel before seeing him."

"And his office undoubtedly leaks like a sieve."

"I can guarantee it," Pharr said glumly. "He knows it too. He also knows—or at least suspects—that we're looking pretty closely at his connection to the case. He doesn't like it, but he's at least agreed to cooperate with our security arrangements."

"Which are?"

"I'm to take you to his office, but we're going up the back stairs, so to speak—not through his secretary or aides. It'll be just the three of us."

"Then if he's the leak . . ."

"Not him, Mr. Carter," Pharr said as they reached the car, a dark green Chevrolet. "He may be ambitious—he may even be weak or be a Communist—but he is loyal to Thailand. He wants this business taken care of as badly as we do."

"But you're still watching him," Carter said. He was beginning to like Pharr.

"Who knows?" Pharr said, holding the back door for Carter. "We could all be wrong about him. I'm just covering all the bases."

Their driver was a youngish Thai national who seemed to look everywhere except straight ahead at the road as he weaved through traffic at a breakneck speed, all the while humming some tuneless song.

On the way into the city from the airport, Pharr explained what little he knew about Guthrie's investigation of Kangting. He admitted that most of his knowledge came from reading and studying Guthrie's notes over the past forty-eight hours.

"He's a big name out here, Mr. Carter, a very big name. It came as a complete surprise to me that Gordon and Carlton were watching him."

"His people could have killed them."

"It's certainly possible—he has the muscle—but their bodies were found about seventy-five miles north of here."

"Do you know Kangting?"

"I've never met the man. He runs in different circles than I do."

Carter laughed. "What have you heard about his daughter?"

"Elizabeth?" Pharr grinned. "She's beautiful, and she's a hell raiser. She'll probably take over her father's business someday."

"That sharp?"

"And then some," Pharr said. "What's your pleasure, Mr. Carter, cognac, scotch, or vodka?"

"You can call me Nick, and a scotch would be fine."

Pharr opened an attaché case, which turned out to be a well-stocked portable bar. "The VIP kit," he said, pouring them both a scotch. "No one knows anything about you, but I brought it along just in case."

"Let's keep it that way," Carter said. "As far as anyone's concerned, I'm the new military liaison just in for a quick look-see. I'm Commander Nick Carson."

"You're going to nail the bastards, aren't you."

"You can count on it," Carter said, raising his glass.

"Best words I've heard in two days, Nick. They were good men. The best."

They passed the Victory Monument on Phya Thai Road, and drove the rest of the way into the city in silence, pulling up behind the government complex shortly before ten. Carter and Pharr went in the back door and took an elevator up to the third-floor office of the police chief. The rest of the floor was dark.

Colonel Trat turned out to be a tiny, intense-looking man with wide-set black eyes and longish dark hair. He was dressed in his uniform, a lot of ribbons on his chest. He met them at the door to his office.

"Ah, Commander Carson, I have been expecting you," he said after Pharr had made the introductions. "Come in, please."

"I had hoped to go directly to my hotel, Colonel. It has been a long flight."

"Most unfortunate, having to conduct business in this fashion. I apologize, but I feel it is necessary," Trat said. He turned to Pharr. "You have booked Commander Carson into the Oriental?"

"Yes," Pharr said, glancing at Carter. This was Trat's

city. It wasn't surprising that he would know where Carter was staying.

"A fine establishment, sir. And I assure you, we will be finished with our business posthaste. Posthaste."

They went in. Colonel Trat sat behind his desk, Pharr and Carter across from him.

"I shall come to the point without delay, which I know you Americans appreciate. I believe that your trip may have been unnecessary. We will have the parties responsible for this most heinous crime—most heinous—under arrest within twenty-four hours. Justice will be swift and sure, Commander Carson. You have my assurances."

"You know who they are?" Carter asked.

"The perpetrators are known to this office, yes. And they most certainly will be under arrest very soon. You have my personal guarantee. So, you see, your trip perhaps was a waste of time."

"Can we know who they are?"

"Oh, yes, of course. When they are safely in custody. But for the moment our inquiries are at—how shall we say—at a very delicate stage. You must understand, a man with your background . . ."

"May I be of some assistance?"

"Oh, no, of course not." Trat waved Carter's suggestion aside, then sat forward a little. "In fact, I would hope that you would return home tomorrow. Or, at the very least, become an ordinary tourist. Enjoy your visit. There are many fascinating sights to see here in Bangkok. But, please, we do not require any assistance. In fact we might even view such activities as strictly illegal under current Thai law. You can understand this, Commander. We are a nation of laws, after all. A civilized people."

"My government may insist . . ."

"I have spoken with your government's representative, Commander Carson. At length. Let me assure you, at length. And we, as two gentlemen, have come to an amicable agreement."

"Commander Carson has been assigned here as the new military liaison," Pharr interjected.

"So I understand, Mr. Pharr," Trat said smoothly, "and I am certain that when the time comes for Commander Carson to assume his duties, he will discharge his responsibilities with the utmost professionalism."

Carter felt as if he were mired in a pool of molasses, talking with Trat. During the entire conversation the man hadn't said a single thing except telling him to back off.

"If there is anything I can do to facilitate your stay here, Commander . . ." Trat said, his voice trailing off.

Carter and Pharr got to their feet. "I will probably stay in Bangkok for only a few days," Carter said.

Trat got up and extended his hand. Carter took it.

"Then I won't be seeing you again until you return at the beginning of next month."

"Probably not. I would like, as you suggest, to see the sights. And then I have an invitation to have dinner with Mr. Kangting and his daughter."

Colonel Trat jerked his hand back.

"I met them recently in Washington, at your embassy as a matter of fact. Miss Kangting is as charming as she is beautiful."

Trat's eyes narrowed. "We are an ancient people, Commander," he said. "We call our city of Bangkok the city of angels. And where angels exist, so does the devil."

"I'll keep that in mind," Carter said. "It was a pleasure meeting you, Colonel."

He and Pharr went back down to the car. On the way out of the parking lot Pharr shook his head.

"You were pulling his chain pretty hard back there."

"If he's the weak link, we'll know about it real soon," Carter said. The warning had been open and clear. His second in less than forty-eight hours. He'd learned way back that if you wanted some action, you pushed a little. If you wanted a lot of action, you pushed hard. He was just beginning, but already he was getting the impression that Kangting was hiding something, and that everyone around him was lending a hand. Billionaire or not, the man had a weak spot—all men did. And at this point Carter figured Kangting's Achille's heel would be his daughter, Elizabeth.

The Oriental was the oldest and in many respects the most luxurious of Bangkok's big hotels. It was eleven o'clock by the time they arrived. Carter registered and had his bags sent up to his room. The clerk handed him a message that had come in several hours earlier. It was from Hawk, and said simply that a reporter by the name of Betty Chi-Doi-Ko, of Amalgamated Press and Wire Services, would be along to interview him. He'd heard of her. She had once worked out of Hong Kong. "Local color," Hawk had called it. A lot of things had changed in Southeast Asia since the last time Carter had been here. She'd been sent out, apparently, to complete his briefing, and perhaps act as background noise.

Carter and Pharr took a table at the hotel's riverside bar and dining area. They each ordered spicy grilled shrimp and a salad. As they waited for their late dinner to come, they had cold beers.

"Does the message say anything I should know about, Nick?" Pharr asked.

"Nothing important," Carter said, pouring the rest of his beer. He was tired from the long flight, but not so tired that he missed the subtle meaning of Pharr's question.

"Colonel Trat will be watching you pretty closely, at least for the next few days," Pharr said.

Carter looked up. "How long have you been in love with her, Ian?"

"What?" Pharr asked softly.

"Elizabeth Kangting."

"I'm married . . ."

"Divorced."

"It's not been that . . ."

"How long, Ian? I'm going after her father. I need to know."

Pharr sighed deeply and looked down at his glass. "It's not what you think, Nick."

"It's a one-way affair?"

Pharr smiled deprecatingly. "Affair may be a bit too strong a word. But, yes, I'm in love with her. Is it that obvious?"

"Yes."

"Hell. She doesn't even know I exist. At least not in that respect. Like I said, they're way out of my league. But a man can dream, can't he?"

"Have you been with her?"

Pharr actually blushed.

"I don't mean thay way," Carter explained. "I meant, have you spoken with her? Have you been to a reception or party with her? Have you been out to their house?"

"Once," Pharr said. "A couple of years ago. They had a reception for American and British embassy personnel. I was invited." Again he shook his head. "I fell in love with her the moment I laid eyes on her."

"Did you speak with her that night?"

"Sure," he said. "We came down the reception line. I was introduced, and she said: 'Welcome to Thailand, Mr. Pharr.' And that was it. But I've heard those five words a thousand times over."

"Nothing else since then?"

Pharr shook his head, and stared out across the water.

"Could you make me a sketch of Kangting's compound?"

Pharr turned toward Carter, his sadness gone. "I can do you one better. We have photographs of the place. There was a big spread in the Bangkok newspaper a few years back. I'll have them sent over here to you."

"Tell me about her—" Carter began, when suddenly a tremendous explosion split the night air, the shock wave sending him backward against the rail at the edge of the patio, the dining table on top of him.

His ears were ringing, but he was conscious of the sound of shattering glass and of things falling all around him. Then he could hear people screaming, and someone was running to the left. He could hear footfalls crunching in broken glass. He could hear the crackling of flames and smell smoke as well as the distinctive acrid odor of exploded plastique.

Carter shoved the table aside and got unsteadily to his feet. The force of the explosion had toppled the canopy that covered the dining area, and had shoved some of the tables and chairs through the big plate glass windows into the hotel. There was blood everywhere. A lot of people had been killed or seriously injured.

Pharr was on his hands and knees, blood streaming from his nose. Carter pushed his way through the debris to him. In the distance he could hear the wail of sirens. People from the hotel had rushed outside to see what had happened.

Pharr looked up. He shook his head.

Carter helped him to his feet. "Are you all right?"

"I think so," Pharr mumbled. "You?"

"Nothing broken . . ."

The side of Pharr's head suddenly exploded, and his body was slammed violently on top of an overturned chair. Just then a powerful outboard motor came to life on the river.

Carter dropped down beside Pharr's body, yanked open his coat, and pulled out the man's weapon, a Browning 9mm automatic. He scrambled to the edge of the balcony, levering a round into the weapon's firing chamber and clicking the safety off.

A long, low powerboat raced past. Carter caught a glimpse of the driver and a second man in the back, who was just raising a rifle.

Carter jumped up, and leading the boat just ahead of its windshield, squeezed off four shots, the first hitting the dash panel, the second slamming the driver away from the wheel, the third missing, and the fourth apparently hitting the fuel tank. The boat exploded with a tremendous *whump*, blowing out even more of the hotel's windows, sending pieces of flaming wreckage seventy-five feet into the air.

Three of the hotel staff raced up behind Carter and knocked him to his knees, grabbing away the gun.

A woman was screaming, and the first of the police cars had just pulled up out front.

One of the men kicked Carter in the ribs, all the while swearing at him in Thai, while the one with the gun jumped back and pointed it at Carter's head, his hand shaking.

"You animal! You devil!" he screeched.

"The men in the boat set the bomb," Carter said, willing himself to keep calm. The situation was very volatile. The man with gun was a waiter, not a security guard, and was very frightened.

"You killed them! You killed them!"

"They killed my friend," Carter said.

Four uniformed police officers rushed out from the hotel. One of them shouted something. The man with the gun turned to look over his shoulder. Carter kicked out, hitting the man's hand, knocking the gun loose and sending it skidding across the debris-covered floor. Then he sank back, the flames dancing in his eyes, the ringing again in his ears so loud he could hear nothing else.

Colonel Trat was waiting for Carter just outside the emergency room of Bangkok's crowded main hospital. There were many victims of the blast, and the hospital's facilities were overwhelmed.

"They say your injuries are not serious," Trat said. He didn't look very happy.

Carter nodded. He felt like hell, as if every bone in his body had been hit with a jackhammer. "Whoever was in the boat set the explosion. They killed Ian Pharr."

"We're still picking pieces out of the river," Trat said. "I'll drive you back to the hotel. The rooms were not damaged."

Carter fell in beside him. They walked out to Trat's car

and climbed in the back seat. The driver pulled away from the curb and headed back to the Oriental.

"This entire situation has become very distressing to me, Commander. Very distressing indeed. You have been in Bangkok barely three hours and with you has come more murder and mayhem."

"The same people who killed Guthrie, Reed, and their driver set the bomb and killed Pharr."

"I do not believe that for one minute," Colonel Trat said, raising his voice. "The crimes are unrelated, totally unrelated. One was the work of bandits. And this business tonight was obviously the work of terrorists who at this very moment are working for a severance of ties—friendly ties, I might add—between our two countries."

"They hung around long enough so that they could verify our deaths."

"Their mistake. And might I add, Commander, that you were a very lucky man, very lucky indeed. First you survive the bomb blast, then the assassination attempt."

"They'll try again."

"Most certainly," Trat agreed. "Which is why I am ordering you out of Thailand. I will speak with your ambassador in the morning. Strings will be pulled, rest assured. You will be on an airplane out of Thailand tomorrow, and your posting as military liaison will be withdrawn."

"And the killers will go free."

"This is my city, Commander. The killers will not go free. Rest assured, they will be behind bars very soon, very soon indeed."

They pulled up in front of the hotel. There were still a lot of police around.

"My men will keep an eye on things here for the remainder of the night," Trat said. "Get some rest, Commander Carson. Tomorrow morning I shall personally drive you to the airport and see you off. We do not need you here as a special investigator, nor do we want you here as military liaison."

THREE

It was very late—or very early—when Carter finally took the elevator up to his floor. Incredibly, the hotel staff had cleaned up most of the bomb damage. By the morning, he suspected, the hotel would be back to normal, including the riverside dining area.

His room was 818, at the end of the corridor. He opened the door, and immediately stepped back, his adrenaline pumping. The lights were on and he could hear the shower running in the bathroom.

His bag had been unpacked, and he could see his cassette player on the bureau across the room. He'd not had the chance to unpack his weapons.

There was no one else in the corridor. The floor was quiet.

Moving carefully, he stepped the rest of the way into the room, checked behind the door, and then walked across to the bureau. In ten seconds he had the back of the cassette player open and the printed circuit board popped out. He took out his Luger, jammed a clip in the pistol grip, and levered a round into the firing chamber.

The bathroom door was ajar. Flattening himself against the wall, he reached out with the toe of his shoe and gently pushed the door all the way open. Someone was in the

31

shower. He could just make out the dim outlines of a form through the shower curtain. A skirt, blouse, bra, and panties lay in a heap on the floor. In the mirror he could see her purse on top of the toilet seat.

"If that's you, Nick, you're letting in a terrible draft," a woman said from the shower.

"Come out of there," Carter said, bringing up his Luger.

"What, like this, now, with you watching?" She laughed.

"Now," Carter insisted.

"Suit yourself," she said cheerfully. The water stopped and the curtain was pulled aside.

The woman was quite tall for an Oriental. Five feet seven, Carter figured. And she was stunningly beautiful, with long black hair that cascaded down her back nearly to her buttocks, small, perfectly formed breasts, the nipples erect, a slightly rounded stomach, and a narrow swatch of intensely dark pubic hair. Her complexion was olive, and flawless. She stood, one hip cocked, one hand holding aside the shower curtain, and her full, sensuous lips half parted in a smile.

"Well?" she said. "Do I pass inspection?"

"Who the hell are you, and how did you get in here?" Carter demanded.

"The name is Betty Chi Doi-Ko, and how I got in here is a professional secret. You look like hell. How do you feel?"

Keeping his gun trained on her, he stepped into the bathroom and with one hand opened her purse. Among other things it contained a Walther PPK.

"ID is in the wallet," she said, watching him. "I left a message at the desk for you, earlier."

Carter took out the wallet and opened it. Her face stared up at him from a standard Amalgamated Press identification card. She was who she claimed to be. AXE. He relaxed, lowered the gun, and put her wallet back in her purse.

"Do you always take showers in strange men's hotel rooms?" he asked.

"Hand me a towel, would you? My goose bumps have got goose bumps."

Carter pocketed his Luger and tossed her a towel. She stepped out of the tub and began drying herself. She reminded him of a cat, her movements slow, precise, and very deliberate. As if the entire world were a joke, and only she knew the punch line.

"Now, if you don't mind, I'd like a little privacy. And then we can play twenty questions. See if we can't figure out who is trying to kill you and why."

"Where were you when the bomb went off?"

"Up here," she said. "Waiting for you. By the time I got downstairs, the cops had already shown up, and from what I could see, all your parts were working." She stopped and looked seriously at him. "You are okay, aren't you?"

"I'll live," Carter said. He turned and went back into the bedroom, where he dug a small bottle of cognac from a zippered compartment in his suitcase. He poured himself a drink, unpacked Hugo and Pierre, then took off his jacket and tie, and slipped out of his shoes. His chest still ached from the concussion of the blast, and a large bruise had already started to form on his shoulder where he'd been hit by the table.

CIA operations were, at least temporarily, at an end in Bangkok. There would be a very large flap out of Washington, but he was fairly certain that he would be kept out of it. Langley knew they were in over their heads here; it was why they had called AXE in the first place. As soon as Colonel Trat started making noises, however, Hawk was going to have to pull a few strings. He just hoped that Trat did not have any suspicions concerning Betty. If he suspected she was something other than a wire service reporter, her sudden association with Carter would raise some uncomfortable questions.

When Betty came out of the bathroom, her hair was wrapped in a towel and she wore one of the hotel's terry-cloth robes. She'd brought her purse out with her.

"Me too," she said, indicating the cognac. As Carter was pouring it, she went to the telephone and dialed for the hotel operator.

"Who are you calling?" Carter asked, handing her her drink.

"Thanks," she said. "Hawk wants to talk to you." She turned back to the phone. "I want to place an overseas call," she said. She gave the operator the familiar number. She took a big drink, then set the glass down and fumbled in her purse for something. "Are you okay, really, Nick?"

"Sore, but nothing is broken. They hit Ian Pharr."

"I heard," she said seriously. She'd pulled out a portable scrambler from her purse, which she deftly clamped over the telephone receiver.

"Did you know him?"

"Only slightly. But he was a good man, if a little young. Had the hots for Kangting's bratty daughter . . ." She turned back to the telephone. "Switching on now, sir," she said softly. She flipped a switch on the scrambler. "You got me?"

Carter watched her in open admiration. She was a pro, no doubt of it. Just as there was no doubt in his mind that she had not been raised or educated in the Far East. Her accent, if she had one, was not Oriental. Chicago, he figured.

"Yes, sir," she said. "He's right here. Just got back from the hospital." She turned and handed the receiver to Carter, then went across to the sliding glass doors, opened them, and stepped out onto the balcony.

"Nick," Hawk rasped, "are you all right?"

"Yes, sir," Carter said.

"Betty briefed me on most of the details. Were they after you?"

"I think so. But I was with Ian Pharr, so they could still have been targeting CIA. They stuck around long enough to make sure." Quickly and succinctly, Carter told Hawk everything that had happened to him from the moment he had stepped off the plane what seemed like two weeks ago, including Pharr's admission that he was in love with Elizabeth Kangting, and Colonel Trat's warning that Carter would be kicked out of Thailand as soon as he could arrange it.

"Don't worry about him, Nick. We'll take care of it from this end. I want you to stay away from the embassy, though, and the team the Company is sending over. As long as we can keep you isolated from them, we might be able to see just who is the target."

"What about Colonel Trat, sir? Could he be in on this?"

"Absolutely not. From what I'm told, the man might be a little odd, but he is first class. He's just what he seems, a cop doing his job."

"Yes, sir."

"Did you mention Kangting's name to him?"

"Not in connection with my investigation."

"Don't. Whatever you need in the way of backup out there, Betty will handle it for you. Our office is small, but she's got a few good free-lancers working for her."

Carter glanced at her out on the balcony. She was smoking a cigarette, staring down at the river.

"She's a good woman, Nick. Her husband was Tommy Bruce."

"Peking? One of ours?"

"Found his body in the South China Sea two years ago. They'd tortured him, but he probably didn't talk. None of our people were compromised. She took it pretty hard. She's been a one-woman army ever since. Trust her, Nick. She won't let you down."

"I understand," Carter said.

"What have you got planned now?"

"If you can keep Colonel Trat off my back, I think I'll pay a social call on Kangting. When we met in Washington he did invite me to dinner. His daughter seemed interested. Might pay to shake him up a little."

"Be careful, Nick. A lot of good men have ended up dead. No finesse, but he's got the muscle to do the job."

"I'll watch myself, sir."

"Do that," Hawk said, and hung up.

Betty came back in when Carter had cradled the receiver. Her glass was empty. He poured her another, and they sat down across from each other, Carter on the bed, she in a chair.

"So, was I given good marks?" she teased.

"University of Chicago?"

She laughed. "Northwestern, actually. Nice guess."

"Hawk told me about your husband. I'm sorry."

"So am I, Nick, so am I. Now, who do you suppose was gunning for you?"

"Robert Kangting."

Her eyebrows rose. "I was given the theory. But why? What would the man have to gain by going over to the Chinese? It doesn't make a lot of sense from where I sit. Does it to you? Am I missing something?"

"I don't know. But I'm going out to see him in the morning."

"You know him?"

"I met him in Washington," Carter said. He told her what had happened at the Thai embassy.

"I call Elizabeth the spider woman," Betty said. "She collects men, and when they start to get close they have a habit of turning up missing, if you know what I mean."

"Her father's doing, or hers?"

Betty shrugged. "Same difference. But if you're going after her, watch yourself. He's got his own private army out there. All pros. Half of them with criminal records a mile long. A pretty tough bunch. But what about me?"

"We mount a surveillance operation on Mr. Kangting. I want to know everything. Every time he sneezes, I want it written down."

"I have a couple of guys who can do the job," she said, thinking.

"Guthrie and Reed may have been watching Kangting when they got hit, so tell your people to watch their asses."

"Don't worry, I will. Anytime you get close to Kangting you have to watch your step." She shook her head. "Even then it might not be any use. A few billion dollars has a bit of clout, if you know what I mean."

"Yeah," Carter said tightly. He was thinking about Pharr, who'd been in over his head. Someone was going to have to tell his father, and Carter did not envy the person that job.

"That was a pretty close call down there, from what I could see," Betty said. "And some pretty nice shooting."

"Thanks," Carter said. He got to his feet. "Now I'd like to get a little sleep, if you don't mind. Tomorrow—or should I say later today—is going to be busy."

Betty looked up appraisingly at him. "Mind if I stick around awhile? I'd like to make a couple of phone calls, get the ball rolling, and then I'll just curl up on the chair."

"I don't need a babysitter . . ."

"I do," she said, her eyes wide. She was putting him on, but Carter decided he didn't care.

"Whatever makes you happy," he said, and he started for the shower. Then he turned back. "By the way, what *were* you doing taking a shower here?"

She grinned. "I was dirty, why else?"

At dawn Carter came half awake when Betty crawled in beside him, but then he fell asleep again immediately. When he awoke a few hours later, the sun streaming in his windows, she was gone.

She'd left a note on the bureau, asking him to meet her for a late lunch, around two, at Chitr Pochana, which was a restaurant on Sukhumvit Road that served authentic Thai dishes.

He showered and shaved, strapped on his weapons, and was down having breakfast by nine. Already the day was hot and steamy. Because of last night's incident, there weren't many people in the dining room. Carter figured a lot of the hotel's guests had probably checked out.

His waiter was just pouring him coffee when Colonel

Trat showed up and charged across the dining room.

"Care to join me, Colonel?" Carter asked.

Trat didn't speak for a good ten seconds. He just studied Carter. But then he finally sighed, and came a little closer. "You pull some powerful strings, *Mr*. Carson," he said, stressing the word heavily. "I know now that you are some sort of cop, and not a naval officer."

"We are brothers, then, it would seem," Carter said evenly. He did not want to goad the man. Just because he didn't want the police involved now didn't mean he wouldn't need Trat's cooperation later.

"Brothers, perhaps, but I think with you here, there will be a lot of trouble in my city."

"Not of my doing, Colonel, I assure you. I'm here merely to—"

"I know why you have come to Thailand, Mr. Carson. And for all our sakes, I sincerely hope you allow me to do my job without interference."

"Exactly my wish, Colonel."

Trat looked at him again for a few seconds without speaking. "I understand a woman spent the night with you," he said at last.

Carter smiled. "I have old friends here."

"Anyone I should know?"

Carter shrugged. "I don't think so."

"No," Trat said. "Take care, Mr. Carson." He turned on his heel and stalked out, two uniformed policemen meeting him at the doorway and escorting him out.

Carter glanced over his shoulder at the other diners, some of whom were looking his way. Trat had focused too much attention on him. He was going to have to move very fast now. Every man had his weak spot. He'd already decided Kangting's was his daughter. It was time, he decided, to begin pushing back.

Carter hired a Peugeot and driver through the hotel, and by eleven-thirty was at the front gate of Kangting's expansive compound on the north side of the city. A burly Western European guard dressed in light slacks and a loose shirt, an M-16 slung over his shoulder, came out to meet them.

Carter lowered his window. "I've come to see Mr. Kangting and his daughter."

The guard looked at him, then at the driver. He wasn't at all impressed. "I see, sir. Did you call this morning?"

"No, I didn't," Carter said. "I met Mr. Kangting and Elizabeth in Washington a couple of days ago at the Thai embassy. Mr. Kangting invited me to visit him when I arrived in Bangkok."

"I suggest you return to your hotel, Mr. . . .?"

"Carson. Commander Nick Carson."

"Yes, Commander Carson. May I suggest that you return to your hotel and telephone. I'm sure that Mr. Kangting's secretary will arrange a meeting."

Carter smiled pleasantly. "And may I suggest that you run along now like a good little boy and tell your boss that I'm here. We wouldn't want to see your little toy gun taken away from you, would we?"

The guard stiffened, but held himself in check. Carter figured the man was strong enough to rip the door off the car if he got mad. But he had nice control. He nodded slightly, then turned and went back up to the brick guard-house just inside the gate.

Carter's driver was clearly nervous. He understood English, and he knew whose place this was. But he said nothing.

The big guard returned a couple of minutes later, the gates swung open, and he waved them through.

"Thanks, buddy," Carter said as they passed, but the guard stood stone-faced. The man was definitely a professional. One, Carter figured, with whom he'd have to deal sooner or later.

The road wound through thick foliage, then over a wooden bridge across a narrow canal, and finally around to the front of the main house, which looked more like some ancient

Siamese palace than the residence of a twentieth-century mogul. Kangting lived well and wasn't afraid, apparently, to flaunt it. A matched pair of cream-colored Rolls-Royces were parked beside a low-slung, fire-engine-red Ferrari. Carter would have bet anything that it was Elizabeth's car.

A pretty young girl in a white blouse and brightly colored sarong, her feet bare, came out of the house, bowed low when Carter got out of the car, and led him back across a broad veranda to the back where she seated him on a deck overlooking a broad lily pond and beautiful Japanese-style rock garden. The sounds of songbirds mingled with the soothing sounds of water splashing over rocks. The air was heavy with the scent of tropical flowers, and the sun shining through the trees lent a dappled effect to the scene.

A young man dressed similarly to the girl came with a pitcher of gin and tonic, poured Carter a tall glass, and then departed.

Carter had just lit a cigarette and taken his first taste—Boodles gin, he was almost certain—when Elizabeth Kangting, her hair pulled back, dressed in nothing more than the wispiest of white string bikinis, a short white silk robe tossed over her shoulder, came from the house. She stopped short when she saw Carter sitting there and came across to him.

"Well," she said brightly, "if it isn't Commander Carson come to pay his respects."

Carter rose. "Good morning, Miss Kangting," he said.

She plopped down in the chair across from his and poured herself a drink. "Oh, do sit down, and don't be so stuffy." She smiled wickedly. "After all, you have been in my bedroom already."

Carter sat down. "I came to say hello to your father."

"They said someone had come to see father. I had no idea it was you."

"Is he here?" Carter asked, looking past her toward the house.

"Oh, yes, but he's in a meeting just now. He'll be out in a minute or so." Her eyes narrowed. "But don't tell me you came to talk to him about the American military presence here. You are military liaison, aren't you?"

"Yes, as a matter of fact I am. But I must admit I didn't come to see him. Not really."

"No?" she asked, obviously enjoying herself. She looked at Carter over the rim of her glass. "No?" she said again.

"Actually, I came to see you."

"Whatever for?"

"To ask you to dinner."

"When?"

"Tonight, if you're free."

Elizabeth started to say something, but then she apparently thought better of it, because she bit it off. She sat back in her chair and draped her legs over the arm, giving Carter a brief but very deliberate view of her opened thighs.

"I could pick you up at eight."

"A date, then?" she asked. "How quaint."

"I know a little Indian restaurant behind the Trocadero Hotel . . ."

"The Himali Cha Cha?"

"Yes." Carter remembered it as one of the better small restaurants in Bangkok.

Elizabeth's eyebrows rose. "But then you've been to Bangkok before."

"Some years ago."

She seemed to consider him a little more seriously now. She swung her legs around and sat up. "I'd like that," she said. "Will you dress?"

"Of course."

"We'll go dancing afterward. I know a great spot—"

"Mr. Carson," Robert Kangting said, coming across the veranda.

Carter got to his feet, wondering if Kangting had merely made a mistake in his form of address, or if he knew something.

"Commander Carson, actually, sir. U.S. military liaison."

"Ah, yes, of course," Kangting said. They shook hands. Elizabeth had remained seated. She was watching to see what Carter would say or do. Her father noticed it.

"I really came to see your daughter, sir. We're having dinner this evening. If you have no objections."

Elizabeth jumped up and pecked her father on the cheek. "And dancing too," she said. "Ta-ta," she said to Carter and then hurried back into the house.

Kangting was a study in control. He watched his daughter until she was gone, and then he turned his gaze back to Carter. "My daughter is a willful, headstrong girl, but vulnerable for all of it."

"And I am a bachelor, sir, with the most honorable of intentions."

"I hope so," Kangting said softly. "For your sake, I hope so."

"Yes, sir."

"We'll see you at seven-thirty for drinks before you two go off?"

"Of course."

"Oh, and Mr. Carson, I would prefer that the next time you come to my home, you come unarmed."

FOUR

Carter arrived a few minutes early at the Chitr Pochana and was having a gin and tonic outside in the back when Betty showed up exactly at two. She was dressed in a brightly colored wraparound skirt, sandals, and a white blouse that was plastered to her skin, the nipples of her breasts obvious. As she came across from inside the restaurant he was struck at how beautiful she was. He rose for her, and held a chair.

She smiled. "I like a gentleman," she said. "They're so rare these days."

They sat down, their waiter came, and Carter ordered a gin and tonic for Betty and a second one for himself. When they were alone again, Betty glanced over her shoulder at the other patrons to make certain they were out of earshot.

"How did you do this morning?" Carter asked.

"I have four of my people in place, including one of them inside Kangting's compound. He's a mechanic, specializes in exotic foreign cars."

"I saw Kangting this morning. Just a couple of hours ago."

"I know. Kangting was interviewing Charlie for the job when you showed up. He didn't see much, but my outside boys saw you coming in, heard you hassling that tub-of-lard

43

guard, and watched you leaving.''

"I'm impressed," Carter said, and he meant it.

"You should be." She took a sip of her drink. "Okay, we're watching Kangting—what have you been up to? Did you put some pressure on him this morning?"

"I think so," Carter said. "I asked his daughter out to dinner tonight, and she accepted."

Betty let out a low whistle. "You really are something else. But remember what I told you."

"I'll watch myself. But if it is Kangting who killed Guthrie and Reed, and then Pharr, I want to know."

"If he comes after you, it might be just because he's a jealous father. It might have nothing to do with him and the Chinese."

"If he comes after me, I'll find out."

She thought about that a moment. "Do you want some backup?"

"No, just keep your people on Kangting."

"What if he makes a move toward you?"

"He won't—not personally. It's my guess that when his people strike, he'll have an airtight alibi. He'll either be out of the city, or he'll be surrounded with witnesses."

She grinned. "And you want Tub of Lard coming after you."

"It'd be a start," Carter said.

They ordered curried chicken with coconut and a lot of vegetables. During their meal they talked about her work with AXE, and how she had met her husband, who'd been an expert agent in the Far East. She'd been born in Thailand, her father an officer in the Thai air force, her mother descended from Thai royalty. In the late sixties they moved to San Antonio, Texas, where her father attended school at Lackland Air Force Base. Betty decided to stay in the States, moving to Chicago and attending school. In the process she became a naturalized U.S. citizen. She worked briefly for the State Department, then at the U.N. as a translator, and finally worked for two years with the CIA. They assigned her to their Hong Kong station, and while there, she met her husband, Tommy Bruce. Later she was hired by AXE, and for a while they had made quite a team. After her husband's death she had taken over AXE's Bangkok office.

"Why not Betty Bruce now?" Carter asked.

"Cover," she said tersely. "Chi Doi-ko was my mother's maiden name. It means 'island of the mountain river.' "

"What about your parents?"

"Dead," she said, and refused to talk further.

Afterward, outside the restaurant, she looked seriously into Carter's eyes. "Watch yourself around Elizabeth Kangting. She *is* the spider woman, Nick, in every sense of the word."

"Will do," Carter said. He watched her drive off, and then got into his car, ordering his driver to take him back to the Oriental.

Carter spent the rest of the afternoon arranging for a tuxedo, and then, armed with a couple of bottles of very good Thai beer, he sat on his balcony rereading the dossiers supplied him by AXE on Kangting and his daughter.

Though Kangting had begun his financial career—or rather, had begun his fortune—by illegal means, he had apparently been dealing straight for so long a time that no one really cared any longer about the early days. He was not only a power in the region, but he was well respected at the highest levels in Western Europe and in the U.S.

Elizabeth, on the other hand, was exactly as Betty had described her: a brat. But a brat with a lot of money, and a penchant for troublesome adventure. She'd been married twice, once to a French businessman, and the second time to an Argentine architect. Each marriage had ended in the death of her husband: the first in a skiing accident in Switzerland, and the second in a boat explosion and fire off the coast of Brazil. In each case the marriages had been over, and in each case Elizabeth had been on another continent with her father when the accidents occurred.

She was a part of the jet set, but her name never seemed to make it into the gossip columns. Her father, Carter suspected, would never have allowed it.

Finally, in the late afternoon, Carter gave some thought to his weapons. Kangting might simply have been guessing that Carter had been armed at his home. But Carter figured that he'd been scanned either at the gate or when he had entered the house. In any event, the scanner had probably detected only his Luger, and had not picked up his stiletto or the tiny gas bomb taped high on his inner thigh, much like a third testicle.

Before he got dressed, he put Wilhelmina and the extra clips of ammunition and silencer back in the radio cassette player, leaving the radio out in the open. He fully expected his room to be searched, although it hadn't happened yet. None of his security measures had been disturbed: specially folded handkerchief in his suitcase; half-open clasp; hangers in the closets at a certain angle; the explosive locks on his attaché case. He guessed that someone would be showing up eventually to look over his things, and it would probably be that evening, when he was with Elizabeth.

Carter had hired his car and driver for an indefinite period. On the way back over to Kangting's compound, the chauffeur was clearly nervous.

"Pardon, sir, but are you a friend of Mr. Kangting?" he asked.

"Good friends," Carter answered.

The driver was clearly relieved. "I am glad to hear that, sir, because the big one at the gate does not like you very much."

"I'll talk to his boss. But if he gives you a hard time tonight while you're waiting, tell him you don't like me either."

"Yes, sir," the driver said.

They arrived at the gate precisely at seven-thirty, and this time they were allowed through with no hassle. Driving up to the house, they could see that the entire compound was festooned with gaily colored lights, and they could hear music coming from the veranda in the rear. There were a lot of cars parked in the front, every other one a Rolls-Royce, a Bentley, or some other luxury limousine.

Carter was met in front by one of Kangting's housegirls and was escorted to the back of the house. A small orchestra was playing a Viennese waltz at the end of the veranda. A buffet and bar had been set up just at the edge of the garden, and Carter estimated there were at least two hundred well-dressed men and women dancing or drinking or talking.

Kangting, wearing a brocade dinner jacket, was speaking with the U.S. ambassador to Thailand and his wife, when Carter crossed the veranda to him.

"Ah, Mr. Carson, welcome back," Kangting said graciously.

"It's nice to be here, sir," Carter said.

Kangting introduced him to the ambassador and his wife. "You are our new military liaison, aren't you, Commander?" the ambassador said.

Carter didn't know if he was in on the deception or not, but either way he was playing it well.

"Not for a few weeks yet, sir," Carter said.

"Just getting your feet wet?"

"In a manner of speaking."

"Well," the ambassador said, "you're starting in the right place. Mr. Kangting is Thailand."

"Yes, sir."

The ambassador and his wife excused themselves and moved on, leaving Carter and Kangting alone for the moment. A waiter brought them champagne.

"Elizabeth should be ready momentarily," Kangting said. "Forgive a doting father, but I had you checked with my friends."

"Oh . . . ?"

"May I apologize for your cool reception this morning?"

Carter inclined his head slightly.

"And may I offer a car and driver for you two this evening? Bangkok can be—how shall I put it?—a dangerous city at times. Bandits . . . hoodlums . . ."

"No, thank you. I know the city. We'll be fine."

"As you wish."

Elizabeth showed up. She was dressed in a striking off-the-shoulder white cocktail dress, slit nearly up to her hip, gold slippers on her tiny feet, and a sparkling diamond necklace around her long, aristocratic neck. Every head in the place turned to look at her. She came directly across to Carter and her father.

"Talking about me behind my back?" she teased, kissing her father on the cheek. "Don't believe half of what Daddy says about me, Nicholas. He is the original strict father."

They all laughed.

Elizabeth took Carter's arm, her touch light, her scent expensive. "But let's get out of here. These kinds of get-togethers are best left to the movers and shakers. They bore me to tears."

"Enjoy yourselves," Kangting said, and he abruptly turned and moved off.

"He'll get over it," Elizabeth said as she and Carter went around to the front to his car.

"Get over what?"

She looked up at him in surprise. "Why, you, Nicholas. What did you think I meant?"

During dinner they engaged in nothing but small talk: Washington versus Bangkok; the weather; sports, of which she loved polo, hang gliding, and scuba diving the most; and about current political stability in the region. Each time Carter tried to steer the conversation around to her father, she adroitly led him away with a bit of outrageous gossip about some American or European movie star or millionaire.

Afterward they went over to the Dusit Thani Hotel on Saladaeng Circle, up to the rooftop nightclub with its magnificent view of the city. A jazz band was playing American music from the twenties and Elizabeth turned out to be an accomplished dancer, outwardly, at least, extremely attentive to him, at times even deferential. It was an act, but she was very good at it, and Carter felt himself enjoying the evening more than he thought he would.

It was nearly two in the morning when, at Elizabeth's suggestion, they went over to the Bamboo Bar in the Oriental Hotel for a nightcap.

"Some of those parties my father throws last all night," she mused. She looked up and smiled, the gesture warm and intimate. "Of course your ambassador and a lot of the others never hang around that long. But I'll bet by eight, when they start serving breakfast, there will still be a third of the crowd left over." She shook her head.

"He evidently enjoys the company," Carter said.

"I think so," she said seriously. "My father has always loved people. But they haven't always liked him. In the old days . . ." She let it trail off.

Only two other couples were in the bar at that hour. Most of the action this late was centered around Patpong Road, with its discos, massage parlors, and strip joints. This city, like most in the Orient, never really slept; nearly anything imaginable could be had, with enough money, at any hour of the day or night.

Elizabeth seemed suddenly vulnerable. An act, Carter figured, but nevertheless he sensed a change. And he softened toward her.

"I've really enjoyed this evening, Elizabeth. We met in pretty bizarre circumstances, all right, but I'm glad we did."

She laughed lightly. "What in heaven's name were you doing out there on the ledge like that?"

"I'll tell you one of these days," Carter said. "And thanks for the help that night."

She nodded. "How about another drink?"

"Sure," Carter said, and he started to motion for the waitress, but Elizabeth held his hand back.

"No, I meant upstairs, in your room," she said, her voice suddenly husky.

"Your father might not approve," Carter admonished with mock seriousness.

This time she laughed out loud, from deep within her chest. "Somehow I don't think you're afraid of my father. It's one of the reasons I decided to come out with you."

"And the other?"

Her nostrils flared and she raised her chin. "Why don't we discuss that upstairs?"

Carter paid their tab, and together he and Elizabeth took the elevator up to his eighth-floor room. Inside, he flipped on the lights, his eyes automatically scanning the room. Nothing, so far as he could see, had been disturbed.

He closed and locked the door, and when he turned around, Elizabeth reached past him and shut off the lights. The balcony doors were open, and enough city light came in so that once their eyes became accustomed to the relative darkness they could see perfectly well.

Elizabeth came into his arms, her lips warm and soft, her body insistent, her breasts crushed against his chest. They kissed for a long time, her tongue darting against his, her pelvis pressed against him. When they parted, her lips were moist, her eyes wide and dark and liquid.

"Do you think I'm too forward?" she asked.

"Definitely."

"Do you think I'm a hussy?"

"Obviously."

She smiled impishly. "Good. I didn't want you to get the wrong impression."

They kissed again, deeply, and when they came up for air, Carter lifted her into his arms and carried her across to the large brass bed. He slipped off her sandals, and then undid her dress and eased it off her body. She tossed away some wisps of lace and lay nude except for the diamond necklace, her lovely skin shimmering in the diffused light.

Her breasts were smaller than Betty's, but no less perfectly formed. Her stomach was flat and her thighs strong, framing a very narrow patch of pubic hair, the rest removed so that she could wear the briefest of bikinis.

Carter kissed her eyes, her nose, her cheeks, and her lips, their tongues meeting, and then he lingered at her neck for a long time, her arms around him, one leg up against his hip.

He took the nipple of a breast in his mouth, and bit gently. She arched her back and moaned.

"*Dai prod*," she said in Thai. "*Dai prod* . . . please."

Carter slid off the bed and got undressed, moving over to the dresser, his back to her, as he took off his stiletto and then the gas bomb, and hid them beneath his clothes.

When he came back to her she opened her arms and legs to him and her bare skin against his felt alive and vibrant and incredibly young and smooth. Whatever Elizabeth Kangting pretended to be, she definitely was an accomplished lover.

She deftly pushed him over onto his back and kissed the nipples of his chest, and then with her tongue traced a delicate pattern down his belly, lingering at times at the scars he'd acquired on a hundred assignments in as many countries.

Gentle Thai music was playing from somewhere outside their window, perhaps below on the street, and they stopped for a few moments, their bodies still intertwined, to listen. Then she rose up on her knees, Carter behind her, her back arched against his chest, and he took her breasts in his hands, feeling them, tracing the erect nipples with his fingers, then running his hands down her flanks to the bit of dark hair. A long, sensuous, needful moan escaped involuntarily from her lips.

"Oh, Nicholas," she said, turning her head so that they could kiss, the position awkward, but somehow she made the move gracefully. "Make love to me. *Dai prod*. Now, please!"

Gently he lay her down on her back, and kissed the inside of her thighs, his tongue rising up to meet her thrusting pelvis. Soon even he could no longer hold himself in check.

When he entered her, she wrapped her legs around his waist, drawing him inside her, deeper and deeper until their bodies were completely immersed in each other's, and they began to move as if they'd been lovers for years, well experienced and knowledgeable of each other's needs and wants, instead of first-time partners. Totally, utterly, Carter lost himself with the pleasure of her.

They made love slowly and deliberately but no less passionately for their expertise, each thrust met by her rise, each pause met by her perfect control. Soon they were at the very edge, and she followed him slowly back away from the brink, knowing that each time they lingered, the next plateau would bring an increased pleasure. Until at the very end neither of them had any control and they totally let go.

"Lord," Elizabeth gasped when they were finished, and she lay back, one leg over his, her eyes half closed, her lips parted as she tried to catch her breath.

Carter reached over for a cigarette. When he lit it, she took it from him, took a deep drag, and then passed it back.

For a while, smoking, he just looked at her lying in the bed, her skin aglow in the city light from the balcony windows. After a while he found that he wanted her again. He crushed out his cigarette in the ashtray on the nightstand, and turned back to her.

This time when they made love, it was slower and even more deliberate than the first time. And, if possible, even better. When they were finished, Elizabeth got up and went into the bathroom, and Carter lay back, his eyes half closed, the memory of her scent, her touch, her body still strong in his mind as if she were still beside him in the bed.

Minutes or hours later, she came out of the bathroom. Now she was fully dressed. She came across to him in the bed, reached down, and gently kissed his lips.

"Time for me to go, Nicholas," she said.

Carter looked up at her. "Will I see you tomorrow?"

"I hope so," she said. "Give me a call. Now, you go

to sleep." She kissed him again, and then got her purse and let herself out.

A minute later he heard the door open. Carter half sat up in bed. "Elizabeth?" he said. But then alarm bells started jangling along his nerves. She could not have come back in. The door would have locked automatically when she closed it . . . if she closed it . . . .

He started to leap out of bed for his weapons on the bureau, but he was far too late.

Two figures dressed in dark clothing, black ski masks covering their faces, had burst into his room. He got the momentary impression of a large, oddly shaped handgun, the sound of a soft *pop*, and something hot and sharp stung his bare chest.

He looked down to see a dart sticking into his skin just above his right nipple, and he tried to reach for it with fingers suddenly too large, and the dart and his chest began to recede faster and faster . . . .

FIVE

Night had never been so long or so dark or so strange for Carter. Yet he was semiconscious of the fact that he was being moved. For a time, until a masked face rose over his, and he dully felt the pinprick of a needle in his arm, he knew that he was in a car or a van racing along a very rough road, or perhaps a dirt track. Some time later—hours or days, he had no way of knowing—he got the impression he might be on a boat, but then again the masked figure rose over him, he felt the same pinprick in his arm, and he drifted off to a dark, dreamless sleep.

There were mountains, he thought. And snow and cold—he'd never been so cold in his life—and finally there was warmth again, and the voices around him seemed somehow less furtive, as if whoever was talking no longer had any need for stealth. And then there was nothing again . . . .

On the morning that Carter awoke from his drugged sleep, the sun was shining directly into his bedroom window. He came around in stages. At first he was simply aware of his own existence, but certainly not his circumstances. Next, he could feel his own body—his head, his arms, his legs—and he realized with relief that he had not been injured, that as far as he could tell, he was still whole and functioning. And finally he became aware that he lay in a broad canopied bed, which he found odd because the room he was in was obviously Oriental in design and decor. A silk scroll on the wall moved with the gentle breeze from his open window. He could smell the odors of pine trees and perhaps horses, and something else—water. Not the ocean, but water nonetheless. He guessed a lake.

He managed to sit up after a while, shoving the covers back and swinging his legs over the edge of the bed, the sudden action causing a wave of dizziness to wash over him. But it passed as quickly as it had started, and holding onto one of the canopy's posts for support, he stood up.

His image stared back at him from a mirror across the room. He was nude, and he looked gaunt. At least three days' growth of beard darkened his face. It was all coming back to him now as the last traces of the powerful drugs left his system. He'd been with Elizabeth Kangting. She'd just left his room when two men in ski masks had burst inside, and shot him with a dart pistol. His hand strayed involuntarily to a spot just over his right breast.

She'd probably been in on it, he decided. The coincidence was too strong. The question was, why hadn't he been killed outright, his body dumped along a country road somewhere? And just where was he now?

He managed to stagger across the room, on legs of rubber, to the window where he looked outside. He was on the second floor of a very large, substantially built house. It was the only structure that he could see, and there seemed to be no fences or walls. If this was a prison, he mused, it certainly was pleasant enough. Down a long path a boat dock jutted out into a large, beautiful lake, beyond which were forested hills that rose up into tall, snow-covered mountains in the distance. Somewhere a wind chime tinkled gently.

He was no longer in Thailand; he would have bet anything on it. Beyond that, however, he had no guess. In three days he could have been taken literally anywhere in the world. He knew of hundreds of places that looked like this.

The door behind him opened, and as Carter turned around, four young Oriental girls, dressed in white, pajamalike outfits, came in. When they saw that he was up, they giggled, and came across to him.

"Ah, Mr. Carter," one said. "We are so glad to see that you are finally awake. We all thought you would just sleep and sleep until winter." Her well-pronounced English startled Carter, and his face registered his surprise.

They all giggled.

They were Chinese; Carter was certain of it. He turned to look back out the window. Chinese! They'd taken him from the Oriental and had transported him north, probably across the border into Laos, and then up over the mountains into China.

He turned back as the girls took his arms and gently led him across the room and through the door into what turned out to be a very large, very luxuriously appointed spa.

They helped him up onto a massage table, and two of them began working at his muscles while the others prepared his bath in a huge cedar tub.

"We were so very worried about you, Mr. Carter," one of the girls said, her powerful fingers kneading the muscles at his shoulder, taking pains not to hurt him where he'd been bruised in the hotel explosion.

"You were fed intravenously until you were awake enough so that we could feed you broth." The girl smiled sweetly. "But then I am quite certain you could not remember any of that."

"Where am I?" he asked.

The girls giggled. "In the People's Republic of China."

Carter willed himself to relax under their ministrations, and soon he was drifting again. After a while they helped him into the exceedingly hot bath, and, all four of them nude, they washed his body. One of them held a tiny porcelain cup to his lips.

"Drink," she said gently. "It will help clear your head, Mr. Carter."

He drank, the liquid cool and very refreshing. Within seconds his head did begin to clear, the cobwebs disappearing, his dizziness and fatigue melting away, and then it hit him.

They had called him Carter. They knew his identity.

"Ah, see? You are feeling much better now," the girl said, putting the cup aside.

They helped him out of the tub, dried him, and then led him back into his bedroom where his freshly cleaned clothes were laid out for him. His suitcase had been brought from the hotel, as had his radio/cassette deck, the back cover and circuit board of which were open. His Luger and ammunition were gone.

The girls left him to dress. He put on his slacks, a light V-neck sweater, and soft, low boots. When he was ready, one of the girls returned. Of course he was being watched.

"I am sure you must be very hungry," she said, standing at the open door. "Captain Cho wishes to have breakfast with you. There is much to discuss, and he is eager to begin immediately."

He'd been taken by the Chinese and they'd done it so easily. Of course Robert Kangting had the perfect alibi: he'd been watched by an AXE surveillance team. He only hoped that someone at the hotel had seen him being taken and had reported it. Betty was sharp; she'd know enough to immediately contact Hawk, though how they could possibly trace him to this place was anyone's guess.

He followed the girl out into the corridor and then down broad stairs to the main floor where they turned right and went to a long glassed-in dining area that overlooked the lake. A slightly built Chinese in an air force uniform, a captain's insignia at his collar tabs, his tie loose, was seated at a wrought-iron and glass table, drinking coffee. He got to his feet when Carter came in, and the girl left them.

"Mr. Carter, I see you've rejoined the living," the captain said.

They shook hands. "And you are . . . ?"

"Forgive me. I am Captain Cho-en Chomo, Air Force Intelligence."

"Foreign service?"

Captain Chomo nodded. "But of course a man in your position would know that our air force handles such matters." He motioned toward a chair. "Please, Mr. Carter, sit down. Our cook has prepared some really excellent Western-style ham and eggs and fried potatoes for you." He smiled. "Of course I had to supervise; the poor woman has never even been out of Yünnan province, let alone to the West."

Carter sat and helped himself to the food. Captain Chomo poured him some coffee.

"So, you feel okay this morning?" Captain Chomo asked. His English was fluent with not even a trace of accent.

"Where did you go to school?"

Chomo grinned. "I was raised in the States. Grade school, junior high, high school, and then Cal Tech for my degree in engineering. I had a hell of a time learning Chinese. I still get dirty looks because of it."

"Where are we?"

"China, of course. Yünnan province. Have you heard of Kunming?"

"Yes," Carter said. It was a city of nearly two million people. He glanced down toward the water. "That must be Lake Tien-Ch'ih."

Chomo clapped his hands. "Wonderful! In addition to your other skills, you are also a student of geography. But naturally a man in your field would know the world. Intimately."

He hadn't seen any signs of the city from his bedroom window. Kunming was located at the northern end of the long, narrow lake, which meant this house was probably somewhere in the south. That meant he was more than a hundred miles from the border with Laos, with another three or four hundred miles to the Thai border. It was a very long ways to go.

"Don't be depressed, Mr. Carter. You will be well treated if you cooperate with us, believe me."

"My name is Carson . . ."

"I do not want to play games. Your name is Nicholas Carter. You are not the new military liaison to Thailand. And although I know you don't work for the CIA or for the State Department, I do know that you work in your government's secret service. Which? The National Security Agency? Naval Intelligence?"

Carter ignored the question. He started on his breakfast, which was quite good. "Why was I brought here?"

Chomo studied him for several seconds before smiling sadly and shaking his head. "You *are* going to be difficult then, aren't you."

"You might try drugs."

"We have. But as you know, we can't make you say anything you don't want to say unless we increase the dosage, in which case there exists the grave risk of brain damage. And we would very much like to keep your brain intact. At least for the moment."

"Torture?" Carter asked.

"Alas, yes, eventually, though I'd personally like to avoid it." He looked away momentarily. "In my dreams I often hear the screams of men I've interrogated. I have terrible nightmares . . ."

"I could kill you right now," Carter said softly.

Chomo turned back, his gaze intense. "You certainly could try. And then what? Where would you go? And you do understand the risk you would be taking. Your next interrogator might not be so kind. He would almost certainly not offer you the same opportunities for cooperation that I am."

"My government will come looking for me."

"Oh, I hope so, Mr. Carter. I sincerely hope so."

"Even now they will be searching Bangkok."

"They have been for the past seventy-two hours. They're very upset, I'm told. Very upset indeed. But that should have no effect on us here. At least not for the moment."

Carter drank some of the coffee, looking at the captain over the rim of his cup. He would have to bide his time, watch for his opportunities. There certainly were guards here, and electronic surveillance. They'd be watching his every move twenty-four hours a day. No matter where he was, he would never be alone.

Captain Chomo brightened. "Well, Carter, tell me about last year's Super Bowl. I was certain that Denver was going to take it. What was it, ten-seven at the half?"

"Ten-nine," Carter answered, and Chomo brightened even more. It was an old interrogation ploy: if the subject refuses to answer the vital questions, ask him something innocuous, something that he will answer. Then the door is open. The subject will begin to get used to answering questions.

For the time being, Carter decided he was going to play along with his captors. Sooner or later an opportunity would present itself.

After breakfast they went outside, where they walked down to the lakeshore. The day was brilliant and warm, though they could feel a slight coolness to the breeze coming down off the snow fields in the mountains. Chomo had brought along a pack of Carter's custom-blended cigarettes. He handed them over.

"Thought you might like these," he said.

Carter lit one, and they started to walk along the rocky shoreline. There were no guards in evidence anywhere, though Carter suspected they were around.

"This place sort of reminds me of northern California, you know. Except of course the air is much cleaner here. Did you know that industrial pollution and car exhausts from L.A. and San Francisco are actually killing the giant redwoods? It's a shame. Magnificent trees. Have you seen them?''

"A long time ago," Carter said. "Do you miss the States?"

Captain Chomo had to smile. "I'm supposed to say no, you know. Decadent, lawless society and all that party rubbish. But in fact I do miss it at times. Telephones that work, decent television programs, football and baseball. Even McDonald's. Silly, isn't it?"

"Not at all," Carter replied. "It is your homeland."

"Oh, no," Chomo said gravely. "I may have been raised there, but this is my homeland. Make no mistake about that."

"Were you a Maoist?"

"No. That was why it took me so long to return home. Mao was necessary to bring us into the twentieth century, but once there, he was an anachronism. It's a shame."

"When did you come to China?"

"Some years ago. But it is my turn again. What were you doing in Bangkok?"

"Getting set to take over my new job as military liaison to the Thai government."

Chomo suddenly stopped. "It was you, then, wasn't it, at the Thai embassy in Washington last week."

Carter looked puzzled.

"The embassy guards shot at an intruder. Second- or third-floor window ledge or something like that. What the hell were you doing up there?"

"I don't know what you're talking about."

"Come off it, Carter. The moment you showed up in Bangkok you went immediately to see Robert Kangting and took his daughter out. Quite a girl. My people said they got very worked up watching you two make love. They thought you'd never finish so that they could get in and do their business."

"Was she in on it?"

Chomo smiled. "What do you think?"

"I think that I shouldn't believe anything you tell me."

Chomo nodded his understanding and agreement. "Makes us even, then, doesn't it?"

Carter looked off across the lake, and then back the way they had come. "You know that I won't answer your questions, so what did you hope to gain by bringing me here?"

"I think you will cooperate eventually."

"And if I don't? If you end up killing me?"

Chomo shrugged. "Your kidnapping is still an embarrassment to your government."

"How so?"

Chomo grinned. "You were the best, Carter. Yet you were taken so easily."

They spent the remainder of the morning in Chomo's ground-floor office that looked north up the lake. The captain had hung a Cal Tech pennant on the wall, along with photographs of his college days in the States. It was a book-lined room, most of the volumes in English, and comfortable even by Western standards, with a sideboard bar, a couch and easy chairs, and a broad, leather-topped desk. Chomo had done well for himself, apparently, coming to China.

They spoke mostly of recent events in the United States, eventually leading Carter to the understanding that it had been at least six years since Chomo had last been back. He seemed hungry, almost desperate for news. But it was all a ploy, Carter figured. Chomo was an expert.

From time to time a question about tradecraft or other procedures would come up, and each time Carter sidestepped any real response, Chomo would shake his head sadly.

"I'd hoped you wouldn't be quite this difficult, Nick," he said.

"We've just begun."

"Yes," Chomo said. He glanced at his watch. "Let's call it quits for this morning. You may return to your room."

Carter got up and left the office. He was met in the

corridor by one of the white-clad girls who had massaged
and bathed him that morning. Together they went upstairs.
She seemed particularly bright and buoyant, and chattered
all the way up in her precise, classroom English about the
lovely weather they'd been having, and about their weekends
in Kunming, which they sometimes reached by boat. At
other times a van was sent for them.

"We need the relaxation among people," she explained.
"It becomes very lonely here sometimes. And there are
times of very great stress on us all."

A pair of thin white coveralls had been laid out on his
bed, and the girl indicated them. "If you would be so good
as to change into those, Mr. Carter. No underwear though,
please."

She went across the room, opened a bureau drawer, and
took out a pair of paper slippers. She brought them back to
the bed and handed them to Carter.

"You'd better wear these. The floors here are cold, even
at this time of year."

"What time is it?" Carter asked. He knew what was
coming.

She looked at her watch. "Oh, it is just a little past noon."

"How about lunch?"

She smiled brightly. "Oh, no, Mr. Carter. You would
not want lunch, believe me. It will be so much better for
you on an empty stomach." She left.

Carter immediately crossed the room and tried the door,
but it was locked, as was the door to the spa. Even the
windows had been closed and locked, a thick wire mesh
covering the opening on the outside.

For the next fifteen minutes he methodically searched his
room, the closet, the bureau, and the bed itself for a weapon,
any kind of weapon, but there was absolutely nothing he
could use. Whoever had designed the room had known what
he was doing.

Two large men, also in the white pajamas, came for him
at twelve-thirty. They seemed genuinely disappointed that

he hadn't changed his clothes.

"Will you get dressed, please, Mr. Carter?" one of them asked politely.

Carter had his back to the wall. He shook his head. The other man pulled out a dart pistol and cocked the hammer. "I am afraid, sir, that this drug would not be so pleasant as the other. When its effects begin to wear off, you will experience a most excruciating pain. And you will lose control of your bodily functions, which is most unpleasant."

The same girl as before pushed past the two orderlies and crossed the room to Carter. "Please, Mr. Carter," she said softly. "This afternoon is going to be very unpleasant for you. But it will be over soon. Please, don't make it any more difficult for yourself." She shook her head. "We are not barbarians."

Carter looked down at her for a long moment, then nodded.

The girl turned back to the orderlies. "Put that gun away, if you please," she said.

Carter quickly stripped off his clothing, including his underwear, and got dressed in the coveralls and slippers. He followed his guards back down the corridor, and then downstairs to the basement, which looked more like an operating theater than anything else. The walls were thick and tiled, the fixtures gleaming stainless steel, the overhead lights very harsh. Captain Chomo sat in a small darkened room on the other side of a thick glass window.

When Carter came in, Chomo leaned forward and his amplified voice came over the speakers. "Last chance, Mr. Carter. I want you to say your last name, and to tell me the name of the organization you work for. Nothing more this afternoon, I promise you. Give me those two insignificant truths, and we'll grab a late lunch and perhaps go for a boat ride on the lake. It's a lovely day out there."

Carter said nothing.

"Get undressed please," one of the orderlies said, while the other laid a thick rubber pad on the steel operating table.

Carter hesitated a moment, but then he complied and was helped up on the table. His arms were strapped down, his knees raised, his legs spread, and his feet strapped into rubber stirrups, much like a woman on a delivery table, ready to give birth.

Quickly and efficiently the orderlies attached electrodes to his temples, to his nipples, to the soles of his feet, and finally to his testicles.

Carter willed himself to relax totally. When the pain came he would flow with it. He would allow himself to hurt, to scream, to writhe on the table. When it came, the pain would occupy his every thought. His *every* thought. Nothing else would be on his mind.

"Now, Nicholas"—Chomo's voice was close at his ear—"what is your real name?"

"Nicholas Carson," Carter said calmly.

The first electric shock came to his testicles, the pain raging through his body, lodging deeply within his armpits, and coming much stronger, and very much harder than he had expected it would be. He screamed, his voice loud and ragged as the pain continued to well up around him until there was nothing in his universe except for the pain.

SIX

Carter's body was on fire. Every muscle ached; every bone was sore. It was as if he had been run over by a truck and dragged for miles over a rough gravel road. He was only vaguely aware that he had been brought back to his room, and he lay for a long time in the darkness, worrying that it was still daylight and his eyes had been damaged.

When he was finally able to prop himself up on his elbows and look toward the window, he could see that it was night. He could see the stars in the crystal-clear sky. It meant he'd been downstairs for at least eight hours, perhaps more. But he didn't think he had talked. He kept hearing in his brain his answers that his name was Nick Carson, and that he was the U.S. military liaison to the government of Thailand. And he kept hearing Chomo's voice in his ear.

The girls came in, clucking like mother hens. One of them pushed a wheeled cart loaded with food and drink. They brought a pack of his cigarettes.

"You are such a brave man, Mr. Carter," one of them said, shaking her head. "But so foolish. It will go on, you know, until you finally answer their questions."

"But no more of this," the one who had been with him that morning said. "Let the poor man have something to eat. He must be starved. He'll need his strength.''

They helped him to sit up, and as one of the girls was uncovering the dishes, another pouring his beer, the one from the morning spread a very soothing salve over the spots where the electrodes had been placed on Carter's body. The relief was instantaneous. When she gently spread his legs, he flinched involuntarily.

"Easy now, Mr. Carter," she said gently. "Nothing has been damaged permanently—yet. I assure you. But this salve will help.''

When she was finished, he did feel much better, and the girls helped him with his meal of beef and vegetables in a wonderful spicy sauce, along with soup and dumplings, noodles and another sauce, and very good, ice-cold Chinese beer. Afterward, one of the girls lit him a cigarette, then went away with the other two, leaving behind only the one from that morning.

She was slightly built and attractive, with high cheek-bones, glossy black hair, and shining dark eyes.

She turned down the lights. "I am called Tsien-Tsien," she said. She unpinned her long hair, letting it fall down around her shoulders, then slipped out of her loose pants and shirt. She was nude beneath, the nipples of her small breasts proud and very dark, the hair at her pubis completely removed, as was the custom among many Oriental women. Though petite, her body was well formed and strong-looking.

It was part of the recovery treatment. Carter shook his head. "I don't think so, Tsien-Tsien," he said, but he had trouble forming the words. His mouth wasn't working properly.

"It is necessary, believe me, Nicholas," she said, coming to him.

He tried to sit up as she pushed him back, but he could not. He guessed that his dinner had been drugged.

"Don't fight it," she said softly in his ear, kissing his temples, and his eyes, and then his lips. "You cannot do anything about it, you see, but your sexual ability won't be impaired.''

Gently she kissed his chest, her tongue lingering at his nipples, and then she worked her way lower. ''Some men are worried afterward that the electric shocks to their testicles will make them impotent. But it is not so. We are *not* barbarians.''

Carter felt a lethargy, and yet he could feel that he was responding. She took him in her mouth and slowly began to move. Carter managed to raise his right hand so that he was touching her shoulder, but he had no strength, and after a while he could feel himself being swept up in the moment, in his pleasure, made even more intense by its contrast to the pain he had endured that afternoon, and it seemed to go on and on forever.

The sun was streaming in his window again when Carter awoke from a deep, dreamless sleep. For a minute or so he did not move, savoring a feeling of relaxation and well-being.

When he finally did sit up in bed, the door opened and the four girls trooped in, giggling as they had the previous morning.

They helped him out of bed and into the spa, where they began massaging his muscles as his bath was being drawn. Today, he realized, was going to be a repeat of yesterday. The morning ritual, the afternoon's clinically detached torture, and presumably his pleasure in the evening.

It was a weakness. In routine comes opportunity, and Carter began his planning as the girls cooed over his marvelous strength, bravery, and powers of recuperation.

Captain Chomo was waiting for him in the same dining room, and they ate breakfast together as they had the day before.

''I trust you had a good night's sleep,'' he said. ''You've recovered your strength. Or most of it. You're a hell of a man, Carter. I don't mind telling you that."

"Carson," Carter said, sipping his coffee.

"Of course," Chomo said. "But even you can't go on with this charade forever. And we do have time. All the time in the world."

After breakfast they went for another walk along the lakeshore. Carter pretended to be a little slower, every now and then stumbling as if he were beginning to have a little problem with his balance.

As they walked he kept his eyes open, especially on the way back when they were facing the house. There were a few horses in a corral behind the house that he had not noticed before. Two Mercedes sedans were parked at the side of the house, along with what looked to be a Volkswagen mini-bus. Down the path at the dock, a sleek-looking speedboat was tied up. They were indeed isolated out here, as Tsien-Tsien had admitted, but getting to Kunming on weekends was not difficult.

"Would you like to take a little rest before this afternoon?" Chomo asked as they came up to the house.

"I don't think so," Carter said. "I'd like to sit down for a while. Have a smoke. Maybe a beer."

"Sure," Chomo said agreeably. "We can go back to my office."

They went inside and settled down across from each other. Carter's beer came, and he smoked a cigarette, drawing the smoke deep into his lungs. He sat slouched in his chair, tired but seemingly resigned to what he knew was inevitable.

Chomo was watching him, his eyes bright, waiting for a sign that Carter was ready to break. He smiled. "You could avoid a lot of pain, you know."

Carter nodded slowly, but then he shrugged. "Sometimes I have to wonder . . ." He let it trail off. He didn't want to come on too strong.

"Yes?"

"It's about Robert Kangting. What does he hope to gain working with you? I can't understand it."

"Mr. Kangting is not working with us. Whatever gave you that idea?"

"I was sent out . . ."

"Yes?"

"A rumor," Carter said. He had definitely whetted Chomo's interest.

"But he is not working for us, Mr. Carter. You and your government are mistaken, although justifiably so. You see, my service has made it *seem* as if Robert Kangting is about to come over to us. And our plan obviously worked."

"If your government believes Mr. Kangting is going to defect to us, they would have to stop it. They would have to send their very best agents to Thailand to investigate this. And they did. Our subterfuge was successful, don't you see?"

Carter had seen all along, only he hadn't believed it was the whole story before, and he didn't now. Was Chomo saying that the disinformation plot had been designed to do nothing more than flush some top-flight American secret service agents out of the woodwork? In that respect the operation had been successful: first Guthrie and Reed had fallen, then Pharr and finally himself. But they had made one big mistake: they should have killed him as they did the others. And it still left Carter's major question unanswered: Just what had the Chinese offered Kangting that the billionaire couldn't get for himself?

"Just remember one thing this afternoon, Carter," Chomo said in a reasonable voice. "You are here with us now, and it is here you will stay. How you fare here, however, is totally up to you. There are no other options."

Carter rose to go. "One option, Captain," he said softly.

"Yes? Cooperation?"

Carter held his eye for a beat. "Death," he said, leaving it unclear just whose death he meant.

They came for him at two o'clock. He'd already changed into the white coveralls and paper slippers, and this time

no words were exchanged, nor had Tsien-Tsien come along
to see that he behaved.

Chomo was seated behind the glass, the same as the day
before, and he watched impassively as Carter got undressed,
was strapped to the table, and had the electrodes connected
to his body.

"Mr. Carter"—Chomo's voice came from a speaker next
to Carter's ear—"two things will be different this afternoon.
The first is that I will only ask one question of you: What
is your real name? The second difference will be that we
will double the strength of the currents through your body.
Your heart may stop, but rest asssured we will be standing
by for such an eventuality. You may die, Mr. Carter, but
not this afternoon."

The first electric shock came across his chest, taking away
his breath, and he could feel his heart fluttering, the muscle
trying desperately to catch up with a missed beat and to
remain stable, out of fibrillation. It had come so fast and
with such intensity that it hadn't been painful, only frightening, very frightening.

"What is your correct, full name, Mr. Carter?" Captain
Chomo asked.

Carter focused on Chomo's voice, and on his face behind
the glass window. This afternoon's session would be even
longer than yesterday's, he knew, because this session was
going to be his last. One way or the other.

The pain at his testicles, when the shock came, was so
intense, Carter's scream caught in his throat and came out
only as a slight breath of air, a tiny squeal. He'd been in
the field for a long time; he had endured a long career of
pain and uncertainty, but nothing he'd even imagined could
have come close to this now. And for the very first time in
his career, he began to doubt if he could handle it.

Another jolt came, this one to his temples, nearly causing
the top of his head to blow off. Without pause, another
burst of current exploded in his testicles, and even before
a scream could form, a massive jolt crossed his chest. He

could feel his muscles involuntarily going into spasm, causing his back to arch off the table so high he thought it would break, and then he understood that his heart had stopped. He could no longer breathe. He could no longer move. But he could think, though the lights in the operating theater were dimming fast. Carter knew that technically, at least, he was already dead. The very last thing he was conscious of was Captain Chomo behind the glass, holding the button that controlled the electric shocks, and then everything was gone.

This time when Carter awoke in his bedroom, he was covered with a blanket and was immediately aware of a great weariness that seemed to sit on his chest like a gigantic weight. It was frightening. It was as if he had just been told he had cancer, or some incurable disease. His body was betraying him. He wanted to jump up, get out of the bed, and go running for someone . . . anyone. But the simple fact of the matter was, he could not. And yet he was grateful that he was alive after having been witness to his own death. It was a curious sensation.

Tsien-Tsien was with him, as were the other three girls. They'd brought the cart of food.

"Nicholas, we were so very worried about you," she said. Carter believed she meant it this time. "How do you feel?"

"I don't know," Carter croaked after a time.

"You must have something to eat now. You need to regain your strength."

Carter managed to shake his head. "No drugs. I couldn't take it."

"No drugs this time, Nicholas, I promise you. Only a stimulant in the beer to make you feel better. It will clear your head, and help with your heart. There still is . . . an irregularity . . ."

Carter closed his eyes and sighed deeply. He could feel some of his strength gradually coming back, but he wanted to play the invalid for as long as possible.

"Nicholas?" Tsien-Tsien cried in alarm.

Carter opened his eyes. "No drugs, Tsien-Tsien. No drugs."

"I promise you," she said, helping him up, propping the pillows behind his head. "Get out of here now, you silly girls," she snapped at the others. "Now!" she ordered. The trio turned and hurried out.

She brought soup to the bed, and slowly, as if she were feeding a small child, fed Carter, blowing on each spoonful so that it would not be too hot for him, wiping his lips with a napkin after each time. All the while she talked to him in a soothing voice, telling him that it would be all right if only he would answer one or two silly questions . . . nothing significant, just minor little things, and everything would be fine. They could go outside together, enjoy the days. Make love in the evenings. Captain Chomo was a reasonable man, she said, a very reasonable man. He would reward cooperation. He would make certain that Carter would be treated well afterward.

"Nothing would ever hurt you again," she cooed, bringing the glass of beer to his lips.

He drank deeply, and within a minute or so he could feel his strength returning; he could feel the ache in his chest disappearing and his head began to clear. He drank again, all the while pretending that he was much weaker than he was, and still confused and frightened by what had happened to him in the basement.

It was just dark outside when he finished eating, and Tsien-Tsien pushed the roll-about cart away. She turned down the lights and began to undo her hair.

"No," Carter said weakly.

She stopped and looked at him.

"Not yet," Carter said. "There is something else first."

"Yes?" she said, coming to him.

He looked up into her eyes. "I want to talk to Chomo."

"Yes, in the morning he will see you—"

"No," Carter said. "Tonight. Now."

She seemed to think about it. She nodded. "I will see if he will come up to see you."

"No. I want to get up and get dressed. I want to go down to his office."

"I don't see—"

"I want a little dignity, Tsien-Tsien."

She smiled. "I understand." She glanced up toward the closed-circuit television camera in the corner. "Can you manage alone for a minute? I will go downstairs to speak with him."

"Sure," Carter said.

She looked at him for a long moment, then got up and left, taking the food cart with her.

Carter made a great show of struggling out of bed and staggering across the room to the bureau, where he pawed through his clothes. Everything was there except for his weapons, which he figured would be in Chomo's office. He got dressed slowly in slacks, a sweater, a jacket, and his soft boots. They'd left him cigarettes. He lit one, the smoke making him dizzy for just a moment, but then his head cleared. He was battered and extremely sore from the torture, but he felt a lot better than he thought he had a right to feel. It was always this way, though, whenever he was about to go into action. His adrenaline was pumping.

Tsien-Tsien came back a few minutes later, pleased that he had managed to get dressed by himself. She took his arm and led him out of the room and down the corridor.

"Captain Chomo is excited to see you, you know, Nicholas. Two questions. It is all he wants."

Carter smiled and nodded. "There is more than that," he said. "More that we have to discuss."

"Oh, Nicholas, I am so happy for you. You are such a brave, wonderful man, you know. We are going to have a splendid time together for the next few days."

Downstairs they could hear the sound of several men talking toward the rear of the house. Carter pulled up short. "What's that?"

"Oh, just the guards. They are having their dinner now," Tsien-Tsien said.

At Chomo's door, Carter looked into her eyes. "Will you wait for me? Upstairs?"

She nodded. "Yes, Nicholas."

Carter knocked once and then went in. Tsien-Tsien turned and went back down the corridor.

Captain Chomo was seated behind his desk. He looked up, a big smile on his face, as Carter closed the door and leaned back against it, apparently too weary to move any farther.

"Are you all right?" Chomo asked, his expression now one of concern.

"A little weak . . ." Carter said softly, and he started to sag.

Chomo hurried around his desk toward him. At the last moment, Carter fell into the captain's arms, and as Chomo tried to hold him up, Carter reached out with his right hand and clamped his fingers around Chomo's throat, cutting off the man's air and crushing his windpipe, Chomo's eyes bulging out of their sockets. For just a few seconds as Chomo's struggles weakened, Carter remembered the man seated behind the window, his finger on the button that had sent the electric shocks through his body. Then Chomo's eyes fluttered and rolled back into his head, and his body went limp.

Carter eased the body to the floor and then stepped back, waiting for the sounds of an alarm to be raised. But there was nothing. Chomo was dead, there was no doubt of it. His throat was crushed. He had bitten through his tongue, and blood covered his mouth and dripped down his chin. Carter felt no remorse. By his own admission, Chomo had tortured a lot of men. It was his job.

Moving quickly now, Carter went around to Chomo's

desk. The drawers were locked. Straightening out a paper clip, Carter had the locks picked in less than ten seconds. He found his weapons in the bottom drawer: his Luger with extra ammunition and silencer, his stiletto, and his gas bomb. He also found his wallet and money and passport and other personal effects.

It took him another five minutes to make a quick but thorough search of the office. His attaché case wasn't there, but it didn't really matter. There was no possible way of opening it without destroying the contents, and killing whoever was within twenty feet of it.

Carter was a lot weaker from his ordeal than he wanted to admit, but he couldn't let that slow him down. Another twenty-four hours and he would have been incapable of any plan of action.

He listened at the door for a moment or two, but there were no sounds from outside, and he eased it open. The corridor was empty. From the back of the house he could still hear the voices of the guards at dinner.

He strapped on his stiletto, then loaded his Luger, screwing the squat silencer cylinder on the end of the short barrel and pocketing the extra clip of ammunition.

He slipped out into the corridor and raced down to the far end to the dining room door. Keying the ten-second trigger on the gas bomb, he waited a full eight seconds, then opened the door, tossed the bomb inside onto the table around which sat at least a dozen uniformed men, and closed the door again. Someone cried out, but then suddenly the room fell silent.

Without waiting to see what had happened inside—he knew what the scene would look like—he raced back down the corridor to the stairhall.

A guard was just coming in the door. Carter raised his Luger and fired once, the silenced shot making a dull *pop*, destroying the front of the soldier's head.

"Nicholas!" a woman cried from the head of the stairs.

Carter looked up as Tsien-Tsien raced down the stairs

toward him. He stepped back and raised his pistol, but he held his fire.

"What have you done? Guards! Guards!" she screamed.

"They're dead," Carter snapped. "Go back upstairs. I don't want to kill you."

"Where are you going?" she rasped.

"Home," Carter replied.

She attacked. Carter managed to sidestep one blow, but then she was on him, a karate chop to his right arm, his hand suddenly going numb, the Luger clattering to the floor.

He managed to shove her away with his shoulder, but she came back at him like a madwoman.

Carter stepped back and hit her with a left hook to her jaw, her head snapping back, blood erupting from her shattered jaw and nose, and she went down, her head bouncing on the tiled floor.

"Christ," Carter muttered.

He scooped up his Luger, checked to make certain that Tsien-Tsien wasn't dead, and then turned on his heel and raced out the door into the night.

He suspected there would be other guards outside, but so far no alarm had been raised. It had happened too fast for them.

Around back, he found the telephone wires for the house and cut them. If they had radio communication with Kunming, it was a wasted effort, but it might slow them down.

Reaching the two Mercedeses and the VW mini-bus, he put a shot into each gas tank, the vehicles going up with a loud roar, flames shooting a hundred feet into the sky.

He raced back to the corral, where he opened the gate and scattered the horses, then headed back to the front.

A single guard was racing up from the boat dock. Carter fired off a shot on the run, hitting the man in the chest and knocking him off into the water.

A second guard was just climbing out of the boat when Carter hit the dock. The soldier managed to get off one short burst when Carter fired, knocking him back into the boat.

The keys were in the boat's ignition. Carter jumped aboard, heaved the dead guard's body over into the water, cut the lines with his stiletto, and started the engine with a roar. Without waiting for it to warm up, he took off away from the dock across the dark water, behind him flames still rising up into the night sky from the burning automobiles, the back of the house starting to catch fire. Looking back, he found himself hoping that Tsien-Tsien would regain consciousness in time to escape the building and a fiery death.

SEVEN

The lake was at least ten miles across at its southern end. There was very little wind, so the water was calm. For some time Carter could look back and see the flames from the burning house, but after a while it was only a glow on the horizon.

They'd be coming after him pretty soon. Someone would have seen the explosions and fires. One of the girls would have gotten on the radio to call for help. Before long, he suspected, the air force would be sending out choppers to search the lake and the lakeshore. They'd be looking for the boat first, and then him. He'd give them what they wanted.

The boat was very fast, but still it took him a solid twenty minutes to make it to the southwest shore of the lake. A long, low, rocky beach rose back into some woods toward the foothills that in the distance rose up into the mountains that ran all the way down to the border with Laos and, farther west, to Burma. He figured that if he could reach the mountains, he would be reasonably safe from any search they'd mount for him. He'd have to travel by night and sleep by day. And he knew it was going to take him at least ten days for the trip, probably longer.

He looked back again as he slowed the boat and approached the beach. There were no other options. He might freeze to death in the mountains, or fall off a cliff in the night, but anything was preferable to what he had already gone through at the hands of the Chinese, and what he most certainly would go through if they recaptured him.

The bow of the boat bumped gently on the beach, and leaving the motor running, Carter jumped in back. There were storage lockers on the port and starboard sides of the boat. The port locker contained life jackets and was unlocked. The starboard locker was secured with a large brass padlock. Using his stiletto, Carter had the lock open in seconds. Inside were two Chinese versions of the Soviet AK-47 assault rifle, along with a half-dozen thirty-round banana clips. Carter grabbed one of the rifles and four of the heavy clips and set them aside.

Next he hurriedly opened the engine compartment, studied the layout for a moment, and then, using the point of his stiletto, worked a tiny hole in the fuel line where it ran past the hot manifold.

Slamming the engine compartment hatch closed, he grabbed the rifle and ammunition, climbed up onto the bow of the boat, and jumped ashore.

In the distance he briefly heard the sound of a helicopter, but just for a moment, and then the noise was gone. He knew he'd heard it, though. They were quicker than he thought they would be.

He dropped the rifle and clips, and hurriedly shoved the bow of the boat back into the water so that it was facing straight out into the lake. He pulled off his jacket, tossed it ashore, and slipped out of his boots, then clambered aboard.

He pulled one of the straps off the life jacket and tied the wheel down so that the rudder was amidships. The boat would head straight out into the lake.

The sound of a helicopter came again, this time much closer.

Carter wrenched the throttle, and the engine roared to life. As the boat took off, Carter jumped up on the gunwhale and dived overboard, pulling away from the boat as it passed him.

By the time he had swum back to shore the boat was already out of sight, but he could hear the engine screaming full bore.

He pulled on his boots and jacket, gathered up the rifle and clips, and headed directly away from the shoreline, picking his way through the rocks and into the trees.

A helicopter swooped low over the shoreline, then headed back out into the lake, its spotlight searching the dark water. At that moment a tremendous explosion lit up the night a half mile offshore, and in the flash he could see the bow of the boat sailing a hundred feet into the air.

Now, he thought, they'd found their boat, and hopefully they would believe they'd got their man. The ruse would only work—if it worked at all—until morning, when they would search for the body. At best, he figured, he'd have a twelve-hour head start. It wasn't very much time considering his weakened physical condition and the rising terrain. But twelve hours was better than no hours.

Buttoning his jacket against the already chill night air, and slinging the rifle over his shoulder, he headed a little west of south, using the stars for navigation, toward his first objective. If his memory served him right, the Yüan Kiang River, once known as the Red River, was about seventy-five miles away. Crossing it would be his first major problem. There wasn't a town or a road within fifty miles.

For a long time as he trudged up and down the hills and valleys, he could still hear helicopters back over the lake. They'd mounted a major search party, and because of what he'd done at the house, they wouldn't give up very easily. When it became evident that he had not been blown up with the boat, they would figure the direction he'd gone, and they would be heading up into the hills after him.

At three in the morning he came to a narrow little stream falling down from the mountains, and he unslung the heavy rifle and bent down for a long, deep drink, splashing the ice-cold water on his face. He wasn't really very hungry yet, though his stomach was rumbling. The real hunger pangs would come later, on the second day, and on the third and fourth days without food, things would get tough. After that his energy level would seriously drop, he knew, just when he would need the most strength to climb the mountains and to ward off the cold.

He thought about Tsien-Tsien as he rewarded himself with the luxury of a smoke, careful to cup the red ash in his hands, hiding it from the sky. Every side had such women, dedicated to their cause to the extent that they willingly gave their minds as well as their bodies. She'd been kind and understanding and gentle with him. But in the end she'd been perfectly willing, and capable, of killing him.

After twenty minutes he hauled himself to his feet, forded the stream, and headed up toward a heavily wooded peak, beyond which he knew would be another valley, and then another hill, and another, and another . . . until he either made it to freedom, or he collapsed and froze to death on some summit.

The land was rising now more steeply, the valleys at times flattening out. He passed terraced rice fields that would be harvested in the fall. Somewhere nearby, he figured, there would be tiny villages, not on any maps, of farmers and their families.

At the crest of one hill he stopped long enough to slowly scan the horizon in every direction. But he could see nothing: no lights, no signs whatsoever of civilization except the occasional tilled field.

By first light, as the eastern horizon was just beginning to turn a pale shade of gray, Carter found himself at the foot of a steep, rocky slope that rose at least a thousand feet. A profusion of pine trees grew around the base, and here and there up the steep hillside. Big boulders, some as large as a house, had tumbled down from the top.

He was tired now, and thirsty again, and hunger was beginning to gnaw at his gut. He found shelter beneath a jumble of boulders that formed a cave ten feet in diameter and three or four feet high. He crawled inside, scraping together some dead leaves and pine boughs to make a reasonably soft bed, and he lay down to sleep.

Once during the day he awoke, his heart racing, to what he thought were the sounds of a helicopter's rotors. But soon he realized he was only hearing the wind in the trees and whistling around the boulders.

He forced himself back to sleep, and he dreamed that he was in the torture chamber at the lake house, the pain in his scrotum so intense he cried out, and awoke drenched in sweat.

The shadows were already very long by the time Carter crawled out of his cave and started the long climb up the steep hill. He felt like hell; his mouth and throat and eyes felt gummy, and every muscle ached. For a while, moving slowly up the hill, his pain took his mind off his hunger and thirst, but later his head began to throb, and hanging over the edge of a ledge that dropped sharply two hundred feet, he had the dry heaves.

When he was finished he lay back in the dark, looking up at the crest, still an impossibly long distance above him, and thought about what he was working for, why he had joined AXE in the first place. Hawk's face swam into view. The old man was there, beside him: "It's only going to work out, Nick, if you make it work out," he was saying. "What the hell are you doing just lying there?"

Carter sat up, found a small pebble, and put it in his mouth, sucking on it created saliva, and the sensation of thirst began to fade.

He got to his feet, glanced out across the valley from where he had come, and then started walking again.

• • •

During that night he climbed to a point where he could see the tree line, still far above him, and the snow-covered peaks just beyond. He found a niche beneath a downed tree and slept soundly, waking only once when his heart seemed to be skipping a beat every other second or two.

He found a stream just after sunset, and he drank until he vomited because his stomach was so full, and then drank again, slowly and carefully. He managed to find some edible weeds at the river's edge and ate a few, pulling up handfuls and stuffing them into his pockets.

For a while that evening he felt his strength returning, and he figured he'd made very good time. He saw no other cultivated fields, nor did he see any lights or any other sign of human activity in any direction.

But looming just ahead were the snow-covered peaks, peaks he was going to have to cross, and he began to seriously wonder if he would have the stamina.

On his fourth day, or was it his fifth—he had begun to lose track—he came to a broad valley through which flowed a wide, meandering river. For a long time at sunset, just as he was starting out, he looked down at the river wondering what it was, wondering just where he had come to, until at last it dawned on him that he had made it to the Red River. He had, somehow, come that far. Seventy-five miles without any real food and not much water.

There were lights on the river, away to the northwest. He had to study them for a long time before he realized they were the lights on small boats. Fishing boats. Fish. Food.

It took much of the remainder of the evening for Carter to make his way down to the river's edge, well below where he had first seen the lights from above.

He drank his fill and then started upriver, crawling through the reeds and tall grasses. Food. It was all he could think about. That and stealth. If he made too big a scene here, his pursuers would be drawn like vultures to carrion. Yet he knew that unless he had food—real food, protein—there wasn't a chance in hell of him making it over the mountains now just a few miles away.

He came to a collection of fish-drying sheds at around two in the morning. They were set up on a sandbar just above the water's edge. He could smell the smoldering charcoal, and smell the rich, greasy odor of smoked fish.

At the edge of the encampment he lay on his stomach, his stiletto in hand, as he studied the layout. It was hard to concentrate. He found that he was salivating uncontrollably. In addition to the smoking sheds, there were three campfires around which he could just make out the huddled forms of a dozen sleeping men. They fished on the river and each night brought their catch here to cure it. When they had a full load they would return to their village. They would be tired now, after a day of very hard work. They had posted no lookouts.

He forced himself to remain where he was for a full five minutes before he moved out, forced himself to calm down, to think out what he was going to have to do and how he was going to have to do it. He had come too far now to be discovered and captured.

He left the AK-47 on the ground, and slowly made a wide circle around to the rear of the camp. He carefully approached one of the charcoal sheds, keeping it between him and the sleeping men.

The shack was made of straw and twigs. Using his stiletto, Carter cut a two-foot-wide slit in the back wall of the shed, smoke pouring out of the opening, and he reached inside. The fish, cut into long strips, were hung on poles. Carter pulled out a strip, then sat back and tore off a piece, stuffing it into his mouth. It was still warm, and very greasy. His stomach rebelled at first, and he almost vomited, but then he forced himself to keep it down, and he ate more, a small piece at a time, until he'd finished it.

A sense of well-being came over him, and for a few minutes he sat there, sleepy and content. But then he roused himself and reached back into the fish-drying shed and pulled out a dozen more strips, careful not to take more than one piece from any one pole.

He ate another two pieces, then stuffed the rest into his jacket pockets. As best he could he pushed the twigs and straw back together over the slit, then crawled away, making the same big circle back to where he'd left the AK-47.

When he had recovered the automatic rifle he looked back the way he had come. No one had stirred. They hadn't heard him. The fishermen had not realized their camp had been raided.

Back at the river's edge, he looked out across to the far shore. It was at least a hundred yards away. An impossible swim with the heavy assault rifle and ammunition clips.

He looked back up toward the camp. Several flat-bottomed boats were pulled up on the sandbank. In the morning the fishermen would see, of course, that one of their boats was missing. The alarm would be raised. Unless they thought the missing boat had simply drifted off . . . .

Carter hurried back to the edge of the camp along the river's edge, and then wading through the water he came up to the first boat, which he gently pulled down off the sandbank. When it was afloat, he hauled himself over the gunwhale and into the boat. He stretched out on the bottom as the boat drifted downstream, moving faster and faster as it was caught up in the swift current.

For a while he was content to simply lie there, drifting with the current. But finally he sat up and looked back the way he had come. He could just make out the fishing encampment in the distance, and then he was around a bend and out of sight.

Slowly he was being swept across the river to the far shore. He found the single, long, sculling oar, fitted it into its slot at the stern, and slowly began to work his way out of the current at a broader angle to the shoreline, sweat pouring down his face. It was after five by the time he reached the far shore and set the boat adrift. With any luck the fishermen would believe the boat had merely been swept downstream by the river and would not report it missing to the authorities. At least not for a while.

He set out again, fortified by the fish, toward the mountains and the borders beyond.

The days melded into one long gray stretch of climbing at night and trying to keep warm during the day. He ran out of fish on his third day in the mountains, when he was at the top of the world. He was trudging through waist-deep snow toward a cloud-wrapped peak still a thousand or more feet above him, when he reached into his pocket for some food. But his pocket was empty.

Slowly he turned and looked back down the way he had come, toward the foothills and the river lost in the night, and he did not think he could go on. His body was finally calling it quits. He had gone as far as he could.

He looked up toward the peak. That far, he told himself. He could go at least that far, and then he would see. It wasn't so impossible a distance. Far overhead he could see the vague line of a contrail through the stars. Some jet far above was heading where? Hong Kong? Hanoi?

One foot in front of the other. That's all. One foot and then the next.

Carter was having trouble breathing. It was day, the sun intensely bright on the snow. He had lost feeling in his feet and legs what seemed like months ago, and yet he knew that he was moving downward. He was no longer climbing. And far in the distance to the south he could see the gray-green of the Burmese jungles.

He heard helicopters, and instinctively crawled beneath

some rocks. He reached for the AK-47 at his shoulder, but it was gone. For a long confused minute he pawed at his shoulder, but the heavy gun was gone. Somewhere, he realized, he had lost it. Somewhere, up on the snow fields of the mountains where he had fought for his survival the gun had slipped off his shoulder, and he had not missed it. Now he had only his Luger and his stiletto.

The helicopters went away after a while, and he pushed on.

There were rock fields, and then forests, and finally a jungle through which the going was nearly impossible. He had crossed innumerable streams and rivers. He had skirted so many rice fields and villages that he had lost all sense of distance and direction. He could have been in Africa or Australia for all he knew.

Except that at night, stumbling through whatever obstacle seemed to be in his way, he had the instinctive sense to look up at the stars to see in what direction he was traveling. For a time one evening, he looked up and realized he'd been going north, the way he had come, and had to reverse his direction. Then he'd adjusted his direction again, confused by what he was seeing. Finally he stopped for an hour until his head seemed to come together and he realized by Polaris—the pole star—that he had been going east, and he altered his direction again to the southwest, toward the Burmese border and eventually the border with Thailand.

There was jungle. There was a river, and then a wide dirt road. For a long time Carter lay beside the road, watching the traffic, mostly military trucks with troops in the back, before he realized where he was.

He got unsteadily to his feet, stumbled down into the ditch beside the road, and then crawled up the other side. A big canvas-covered truck was coming down the road, and he began waving his arms.

"*Dai prod*!" he shouted. "*Dai prod*! Please! Please help me!"

And then he was falling face first into the dirt road as the Thai army truck ground to a halt and the troops poured out, their guns trained on him. "*Dai prod*," he said softly. "Please." He'd made it.

EIGHT

Frostbite, a touch of snow glare damage to the eyes, dehydration, and a few gastric problems because of the improperly cured fish. "Worms, too, for all I know at this point," the doctor said at the American Hospital.

Carter had been picked up about seventy miles into Thailand from the Burmese border, babbling something about Betty Chi Doi-ko. He'd been carrying, besides his own weapons, three clips of AK-47 ammunition.

One of the Thai soldiers who'd found him, the doctor told Carter, nearly opened fire, but their commander had the sense to report to his superiors. Colonel Trat was contacted, and the order was given for Carter to be brought immediately by chopper down to Bangkok.

That was two days ago. They'd moved him right away to the American Hospital where Betty felt the security would be better.

Carter was aware of none of that until this moment, looking up at the doctor.

"How do you feel, Commander Carson?" the doctor was asking.

"I've felt better," he said. He felt detached from his body. They'd probably given him painkillers, but his mind was clear. "Any permanent damage?"

"None," the doctor said. "But we're curious about what appears to be burn marks at your temples, your chest, and your testicles."

"You don't want to know, Doctor, believe me," Carter said. "Is Miss Doi-ko here this morning?"

"Yes, sir, she is. But Colonel Trat had requested to speak with you the very moment you were awake. He's outside now."

Carter motioned the doctor a little closer. "How is security here?"

The doctor started to shrug.

"My life may depend on it."

"Miss Doi-ko has seen to it from what I'm told. You're safe here, Commander. Rest assured."

"What about my . . . things?"

"If you mean your weapons, I believe Colonel Trat may know something. Shall I send him in?"

"Please," Carter said.

The doctor left, and Colonel Trat came in, a bemused expression on his face. He pulled a chair over to Carter's bedside. "So, how are you feeling this morning?"

"Unprotected."

"I understand you decided to take a little hike up-country."

"Red China."

Colonel Trat's eyes widened. He was clearly impressed. "Whatever were you doing up there? And just how did you get there in the first place?"

"I was captured."

"Right here, in Bangkok, under my nose? Shocking! And then you were spirited away to China?"

"And questioned, and tortured," Carter added.

"But why?"

"I was with Elizabeth Kangting just before I was taken. She was in my hotel room. When she left, she didn't allow the door to slam shut and lock. They came in right after her."

"What are you saying, Mr. Carson?"

"That we watch Robert Kangting."

Trat smiled and shook his head. "You have been to visit with the Chinese Communists, or so you say, and you are found wandering around in the north country. Next you will try to tell me that you walked over the mountains from—" Something in Carter's eyes stopped the colonel in mid-sentence.

"I would like my Luger and my stiletto returned to me," Carter said.

"What does Robert Kangting have to do with your getting captured?" Trat demanded.

"Maybe nothing. But we must watch him."

"I don't know . . ."

"My people already are."

Trat sucked in his breath. "I will see what I can do, Mr. Carson. It is all I can say."

"My weapons."

Trat hesitated a moment, but then he took Carter's Luger, extra clip, silencer barrel, and stiletto out of his jacket pocket and placed them on the night table. "Not military weapons," he said. "Hateful-looking things. We had to have them cleaned and oiled. They were in terrible condition."

"Thanks," Carter said. "I appreciate it."

"You walked from China," Trat said softly. "And what happened to the AK-47 for which you carried ammunition?"

"I don't know," Carter said. "I lost it somewhere in the mountains."

"I see," Trat said, getting up. "Get well, Mr. Carson, and we will talk of this matter again." He turned and left the room.

Carter heard someone talking urgently in the corridor, and then Betty burst into the room, took a long look at Carter, then blocked the door with the chair and came across to him, carefully kissing his forehead, his cheeks, and then finally his lips, her touch lingering.

"You look like hell, you know," she said.

"Has Hawk been told?"

"I called him as soon as they picked you up. Where were you, Nick? Where have you been?"

"China. And Kangting, according to them, is innocent. They were using him as unwitting bait."

"You walked over the the mountains?" she asked, incredulous.

"You got it," Carter said. "How secure is this place?"

"Not very," she admitted. "I'm getting you out of here tonight. We'll go to a place I know just north of Bangkok. No one will expect you to be there."

"They're going to try for me again."

"But you don't believe Kangting is innocent?"

"I don't know, Betty. I don't think so. I heard him talking with the Chinese at the Thai embassy in Washington. They were definitely making him an offer he couldn't refuse. Whatever—"

"How'd they get you, Nick?" she cut in, her voice soft.

He looked up into her eyes, and told her everything that had happened between him and Elizabeth Kangting—not in detail, but enough so that she understood what had happened that night. "A minute later they came into my room and shot me with a dart pistol. Fast-acting drug. Next thing I knew I was across the border."

"It's been more than two weeks, Nick. A lot of people had given you up for dead."

"Not you?"

"Not me, or Hawk. He said it would be only a matter of time before you returned. But he initiated a worldwide AXE search. Very quiet but very effective."

"They wouldn't have found me where I was."

Her eyes narrowed. "There was a minor fire and a couple of explosions south of Kunming last week. It was picked up on our satellite? You?"

"Yes," Carter said. "Betty, what has Kangting been up to in my absence?"

"Nothing unusual. The man has been back and forth to

Rangoon twice, and has held two more parties at his house, but he's done nothing out of the ordinary.''

"How about the CIA?''

"They've sent out a Crisis Management team. It's being run by Bob Mills, who's supposed to be pretty good.''

"I've heard of him.''

"He has your name. He wants to talk to you.''

"Does he know about Kangting? About our surveillance?''

"I don't know, Nick. But he's pretty sharp, and he seems to have the connections. He brought some good people with him. Apparently they've done this sort of thing before and are good at picking up the pieces.''

"Have you spoken with him?''

Betty shook her head.

"I'd better, then. I don't want his people getting in the middle of something. A lot of good people could get hurt.''

"When do you want to see him?''

"Right away.''

"Here?''

"Might as well,'' Carter said.

Over the strenuous objections of his doctor, Carter got out of bed after lunch, put on a hospital robe and slippers, and left his room, taking the elevator up to the fourth-floor doctors' conference room that Betty had arranged for his meeting with Bob Mills. He had stuffed his Luger in his robe pocket. This time he wasn't taking any chances. The Chinese would be mad as hell. It would not be at all difficult for them to slip someone into the hospital, onto the staff. From now on he was going to have to watch himself.

He was winded and a little weak by the time he let himself in. Bob Mills was a tall, well-built man, dressed in tan slacks and a khaki safari jacket. He'd been looking out the window down at the busy street. He turned around. "You must be Carter."

"And you're Mills," Carter said, crossing to him. They

shook hands and sat down across from each other.

"I understand you had a hell of a time of it up-country," Mills said. Carter found that he instantly liked the man. There was a no-nonsense air about him. A professional. His job, apparently, was to come to CIA stations that had been decimated for one reason or another, and put the pieces back into some semblance of working order. Just by looking at him Carter had a feeling the man was good at his job. He wasn't going to be put off by anything but the truth.

"The People's Republic, actually," Carter said.

Mills's eyebrows rose. "How'd you get out?"

"Walked."

"I see. What did they learn?"

"Not much. They already knew my name, and they guessed that I worked for someone other than you guys. They didn't pull anything else out of me. There wasn't enough time."

Mills thought about it for a moment, then nodded. "Was it related to our troubles?"

"Directly," Carter said. "And I expect Robert Kangting is involved, though at this moment I couldn't say exactly how."

Again Mills held his tongue, thinking about what he'd been told. "Where do we go from here?" he asked at length.

"You continue doing what you're doing, and put your station back together. In the meantime I have people watching Kangting. I'll be putting some pressure on him. We'll see what happens."

"If he is working with the Chinese, he won't be an easy man to talk to, not after what you've done. Anything else we can do for you?"

"How many people have you got with you?"

"Six."

"Are they any good?"

"What have you got in mind?"

"It might get a little warm. Kangting has his own army."

"Two of my people are administrators, technicians. The

other four are very good." Mills took out a slip of paper and wrote a telephone number on it, and handed the slip to Carter. "You can reach me twenty-four hours a day here. We'll be ready."

"Could be your biggest job might simply be staying out of the way."

"We've done that before too, Carter," Mills said. He got to his feet. Carter followed suit and they shook hands. "How can I reach you?"

"Through Betty Chi Doi-ko. Amalgamated Press. And that, Mills, is for you only. Period."

"Got it," Mills said. He looked critically at Carter, then nodded. "Good luck, then."

"Thanks."

Colonel Trat had placed a guard on Carter's door. In the afternoon he got a few hours of sleep, and by seven, when Betty showed up for him, he felt sore but definitely much stronger. His feet, which had been badly frostbitten, were still giving him some problems, though.

The police guard did not want Carter to check out of the hospital, but a quick telephone call to Colonel Trat convinced him otherwise.

Carter and Betty, both dressed in hospital whites, slipped unnoticed out a rear loading entrance and into the back of a windowless van. They were whisked across the city, then out past the Thai National Museum and Emerald Buddha and Palace. Their driver was one of Betty's Amalgamated Press people who had not so far been involved with the Kangting surveillance. He knew nothing about the operation except that he was to keep his eyes open and his mouth shut.

"Did we pick up a tail?" Betty asked him at one point.

"We're clean," the young man said.

A half hour after they crossed the Chao Phraya River, they pulled off the highway and bumped down a narrow dirt road that ran about three miles into the jungle, ending at a tall wire mesh fence. Their driver hopped out, unlocked the gate, swung it back, and then drove through, stopping and relocking the gate before they continued. The road went another few hundred yards into the jungle, finally opening into a narrow clearing in which a beautiful house sat at the edge of a small stream. Soft lights shone from inside.

"Whose place is this?" Carter asked, getting out with her.

"Tommy's brother's."

"I didn't know he had a brother."

"Not many people do. We'll be safe here."

Betty dismissed their driver, who turned around in the driveway and headed back to Bangkok.

"How about transportation?" Carter asked as they walked up to the house.

"There are a couple of cars around back."

"Staff?"

She shook her head. "We're alone here, Nick. Completely alone."

The house was very large, long and low, the back almost completely open to the stream and gently lit gardens. It was beautiful, and very peaceful. The sound of the gently running water could be heard throughout the house.

"I bought you a few things in town today," Betty said, pouring them a drink at a sideboard in the expansive living room. "I had to guesstimate on the sizes, but they'll probably fit."

Carter went out onto the broad veranda and looked down at the water. She brought out their drinks and a pack of cigarettes.

"Thanks," he said. "I want to call Hawk, then—"

"Finish your drink first, and take a deep breath. Kangting isn't going anywhere, and neither are the Chinese. My people will call here if anything comes up."

"Are they still watching his compound?"

"I put two of them on Kangting when he went to Rangoon. They should be getting back later tonight. I wanted them to stick around to see what happened after he left."

"And?"

"I haven't heard from them yet. But they'll be checking in sooner or later."

Betty had taken off her hospital coat. Beneath it she wore a light summer dress and sandals, her shoulders and legs bare. After Elizabeth Kangting and Tsien-Tsien, and everything that had happened to him, she was indeed a sight for sore eyes. He didn't have to pretend with her, didn't have to play games, he could be completely honest, be himself, and it was very pleasant.

He raised his glass. "Thanks for not giving up on me these past two weeks."

They touched glasses.

"Tommy taught me patience," she said softly.

"And love?"

"That too," she said, her eyes steady on his. "He taught me always to be watchful for the golden opportunity. And when it came, never let it get by, because it might never come again."

Carter put down his drink and cigarette, and took her drink from her hand and set it down. He took her into his arms and she came willingly. They looked into each other's eyes for a long time before Carter kissed her, gently at first, and then with more feeling.

After a long time they parted and she sighed deeply. "Oh, Christ," she said. "I forgot what it was like."

Carter smiled.

"Don't do this if you're going to hurt me, Nick," she said.

"I'm not."

"I don't think I could stand it."

"Whatever comes will come, Betty. Beyond that I can't promise you a thing."

"You're trouble," she said. "Even worse than Tommy." She turned away. "Damn," she muttered. "Damn! What is wrong with me?"

Carter took her chin and gently turned her lips back to his, and they kissed again. This time when they parted, her eyes were moist. She pushed away from him, stepping back.

"Damn you," she whispered hoarsely.

Carter said nothing.

She motioned toward the living room. "The scrambler is set up on the phone. Hawk is waiting for your call." She looked at him for another long moment or two, then turned and disappeared across the living room.

Carter finished his drink and cigarette, then went into the living room, where he dialed Hawk's special number on Dupont Circle in Washington, D.C.

It was about nine in the morning there. Hawk answered on the first ring, his voice, as usual, gruff. "Yes?"

"It's me," Carter said.

"Are you in one piece?"

"Yes, sir."

"You met with Bob Mills."

"Yes, sir. He's a good man."

"That he is. Is the situation stable for the moment?"

"Just barely, sir. But all hell is going to break loose very soon. I'm going to see Kangting again, I hope within the next twenty-four hours."

"Is it him after all?"

"The Chinese denied it, but I have a hunch . . ."

Hawk had worked with Carter long enough to have a healthy respect for his hunches. He'd also known Carter long enough to have complete faith in him.

Carter told his boss everything that had happened to him from the moment he'd gone out to Kangting's house to pick up Elizabeth for their date until he awoke in the hospital back in Bangkok. When he was finished Hawk was silent for a long time.

"It was too pat," Carter said, after a while. "There was no good reason for Chomo to have told me that story about Kangting being merely the unwitting bait."

"I agree, Nick. What disturbs me is that they knew your name."

"But not about AXE."

"Not the name, perhaps, but they are aware that there is

some other agency, something other than the CIA or the NSA, and that you might be working for it. I think you were their specific target all along.''

''I think there's more to it than that. Kangting is definitely involved. But how, I don't know.''

''Are you up to it, Nick? Do you want help?''

''Beyond Betty and her staff, no. They want me, and I want them to come after me. This time it won't be quite so easy for them.''

''All right,'' Hawk said, the two simple words his vote of continued confidence. ''Watch yourself.''

''Yes, sir. And thank you.''

Carter hung up and switched off the scrambler. He retrieved his glass from the veranda, and at the sideboard poured himself another drink and lit a cigarette from the pack Betty had left for him.

Back again out on the veranda, the night particularly warm and pleasant after his ordeal, he stretched out on a chaise longue and, drink in hand, lay back and closed his eyes, smelling the tropical scents rising from the stream and the jungle, listening to the night sounds of birds and insects and frogs.

He had to learn what Kangting's relationship was with the Chinese, and what it was they were offering him. He kept coming back to the same thing over and over again, and each time he came up against a blank wall.

He let his mind drift, for a time unaware of his surroundings, thinking instead about Kangting in terms of the man's vast wealth as well as his background.

Stolen drugs, and then opium. The man, at least in his past, had not been above crime. And it was said men never change, not really, not fundamentally.

So what was Kangting after?

Something moved to his left. He opened his eyes and looked up. Betty stood at the far end of the veranda where she had emerged from what apparently was the bedroom. She was nude, her hair up, her body outlined in the dim

light. He thought how much like a princess, like royalty,
she looked.

And then he had it. Suddenly he knew exactly what the
Chinese had promised Kangting. And he was amazed that
he hadn't realized it before.

NINE

"Nick?" Betty said softly.

Carter's mind was seething with what he thought he had just figured out. The Chinese had offered Kangting the colony of Hong Kong. In 1997, when the British lease expired, the Chinese would take it over. But they would need someone capable of running the city-state. Who better than a man such as Robert Kangting? It was the one thing the People's Republic could offer him, that even as a billionaire he could not get for himself. It really could be the answer. Robert Kangting was going to be made king of Hong Kong, and for that he'd do almost anything.

Betty came out onto the veranda. "I'll take my chances," she said.

Carter looked up out of his thoughts. He was going to go after Kangting. But not now. Not yet. First he wanted to tell Hawk, and then he knew he would need more rest. Perhaps a few days, so he could regain more of his strength. He still felt dangerously weak.

Betty was looking at him, her eyes sparkling, her lips parted. The nipples on her breasts were erect. She seemed a little breathless.

"Are you sure?" he asked.

She hesitated just a moment longer, then smiled and came to him on the chaise. "Oh, shut up," she said. "You talk too much."

Her body was warm in his arms, her lips soft on his. There was an urgency to her, as if she wanted to make love immediately, before she lost her nerve.

"Nick, make love to me now. Please," she said into his ear. She unbuttoned his shirt and pulled it down over his shoulders, then kissed his neck, and his chest, soft moans escaping from the back of her throat.

She sat up straight, her legs straddling him, and he caressed her breasts, her back arching, her head thrown back, her eyes closed.

He slowly ran his hands up her thighs to her hips, and she moved against his hardness, now barely able to control herself.

Carter moved her off his legs, and laid her back on the chaise as he got up and began getting undressed. Her legs were spread and she was reaching out for him . . . .

The telephone in the living room rang. At first she didn't hear it.

"Nick, please! For God's sake . . ."

The telephone rang a second time. She glanced toward the living room and groaned.

"Are you expecting anyone?" Carter asked.

She sat up. The phone rang again. "The office," she said. "They know I'm out here. It's probably something about Kangting."

"You'd better get it."

She smiled as the phone rang again. "Don't shut your motor off, Nick," she said. "Mine's just in neutral for the moment."

She got up and went into the living room, and caught the phone on the fifth ring. "Yes?" she said irritably, but then she stiffened and looked back toward Carter.

"When?" she snapped into the phone, her manner suddenly brisk and very businesslike. She nodded. "I'll be right in. We'll decide then if we're going to get the Rangoon police in on it.''

She crashed the phone down.

"What happened?"

"My two people in Rangoon."

"The ones who followed Kangting there?"

"Right," she said. "Their bodies were discovered in a parked car out at the Turf Club. Shot to death. Point-blank range to the backs of their heads. Looked like an execution."

She started toward the bedroom.

"I'll get dressed and go with you," Carter said, starting after her.

She turned back. "I'll only be gone a couple of hours, Nick. There's really nothing you can do. Stay here and get some rest. I'll be back around midnight or so." She smiled a little sadly. "Maybe we can pick up where we left off."

She went into the bedroom and started to get dressed. Carter followed her.

"I think I know what the Chinese offered Kangting," he said.

"What?" she asked, slipping into her panties and then into a pair of slacks.

"Hong Kong."

She stopped and turned to face him. "What?"

"Hong Kong reverts to the Chinese in 1997. They're going to take over, and they're going to need someone to run it for them."

"You're right!" she said excitedly. "It fits!"

"It's the only thing they could have offered him."

"The bastard," she said. She hurriedly finished dressing. "There's food in the kitchen if you're hungry. Get some sleep, and when I get back we'll figure out just how we're going to handle Kangting."

"I'm going to call Hawk. But I think we're off this case. They'll handle it diplomatically."

"They certainly aren't going to arrest him."

"I don't think so."

"The bastard!" she said again vehemently. She kissed Carter on the cheek, and then let herself out. A minute or so later he heard a car start up, and then she was heading down the driveway and the house fell silent.

A lot of assignments in the past had ended up this way, he thought, lighting another cigarette. He walked to the phone and was soon connected with Hawk's Dupont Circle number. Many assignments were never wrapped up in a neat little bundle. Often there were loose ends and dissatisfaction as the only rewards. The politicians got involved and "expediency" became the byword. To hell with justice.

Smitty of Operations answered. "Yes?"

"It's me. Is Hawk available?"

"He's at the White House speaking with the President, Nick. What've you got?"

"When will he be back?"

"I don't know. A couple of hours, maybe longer. He was going over to the Pentagon afterward. Should we call him?"

"No," Carter said. "Have him call me here." He glanced at the phone's dial and read off the number.

"How's it going?" Smitty asked.

"I think we're finished here."

"Hawk will be glad to hear it. As soon as he comes in, I'll give him your message. And congratulations."

"Yeah," Carter said absently, and he hung up.

He stood there in the living room thinking for a moment. Kangting had taken a big chance in having had the two AXE men killed. He'd gone to Rangoon and they'd followed him. Their deaths were too coincidental for Kangting to think that suspicion wouldn't be centered on him.

Or, Carter wondered, was he missing something?

He went into the big kitchen and fixed himself a sandwich. He opened a bottle of cold beer and took his food back out to the veranda.

Betty was right, though; he should be getting some sleep. Kangting wouldn't be going anywhere soon, and if Washington did decide to handle it from this point on, he would be going home. Other assignments would be waiting for him.

But it was hard to shut down. He'd known Guthrie and Reed only by reputation, but he had been with Pharr when the man had been gunned down. Someone would have to pay for that. For that, and for what had happened to him in China. And for the two AXE legmen dead in Rangoon. Those things could not be written off simply because Kangting was a wealthy man.

For a long time, sitting back in the chaise, a tray with his beer and sandwich resting in his lap, Carter let his mind drift with the sounds of the running stream. China seemed like a million miles away and a thousand years ago. And yet it had really happened; he still had the aches and pains, and a smoldering resentment against Kangting.

Another thought struck Carter and he slowly sat up. The killing of the two AXE men in Rangoon would be laid at Kangting's doorstep. The billionaire would have to know that. But he didn't seem to care. Was it possible, Carter wondered, that Kangting was getting set to take off? Was he getting set to defect to China to wait out his rise to the throne of Hong Kong? Or was there something even more sinister going on here?

Carter put his meal aside and went back into the living room. He dialed the AXE number in Bangkok, which was answered on the first ring by a young woman. "Amalgamated Press."

"This is Carter. Let me speak with Betty."

"Mr. Carter, we were just getting set to call out there again. She is not here, sir. How long ago did she leave?"

Carter glanced at his watch. "Two hours ago. I'm on my way in. Don't do anything until I get there."

"Yes, sir," the girl said, and Carter slammed down the phone.

In the bedroom he found the clothing that Betty had picked up for him. She had an excellent eye for men's sizes—everything fit. He dressed in a pullover shirt and sportcoat, a light pair of slacks, and loafers. He strapped on his Luger and stiletto and let himself out of the house, making it around back to the garage at a run.

A big Mercedes sedan was parked next to an empty stall, the keys in the ignition. He climbed behind the wheel, started the engine, and headed down the dirt road. A third key on the ring fit the lock in the gate. Carter let himself through, hurriedly locked up again, and made the highway leading into town just at midnight.

It was possible, he thought, that she had had car trouble, or that she had been in an accident, but he knew in his heart of hearts that that wasn't the case. Bangkok was her town. She knew her way around. If something had happened, she would have telephoned him out at the house or called her office.

He made the forty-minute drive in a little over twenty minutes, pulling up behind the Siam Intercontinental Hotel on Rama Street where AXE maintained its suite of offices.

A portion of the staff here, as in all other AXE offices worldwide, were engaged in the legitimate gathering of news for Amalgamated Press and Wire Services. They did double duty as the eyes and ears for AXE operations.

The office was on an emergency footing. Everyone had been called in. Thomas Lee, the number two man behind Betty, looked up from a teleprinter when Carter came in.

"Carter?" he asked.

"What have you found out?" Carter asked, crossing the busy room to him. Three of the staffers were speaking on telephones, and two others were manning the wires.

Lee pulled him aside. "We found her car around front in the hotel's parking lot ten minutes ago. It could have been there all along, though; no one saw a thing."

"Have you called Colonel Trat? Reported her missing?"

"Not yet. You asked us to wait," Lee said. Carter's Killmaster status pulled a lot of weight.

"How about your people at Kangting's compound?"

"Charlie Knell is working inside as a mechanic, and Don Tak is on the outside. We haven't heard a thing from them in three hours."

Carter thought about it for a moment.

"Is it Kangting after all, Mr. Carter?"

"Looks like it."

"Why?"

"Later," Carter replied tersely. "I want you to try to get hold of Hawk for me. He was at the White House earlier, and then he was going over to the Pentagon. When you reach him, tell him what's happening here, and that we think Kangting has taken Betty. Tell him I'm going to contact Colonel Trat, as well as Bob Mills, and then I'm going in after her."

Lee's eyes had opened wider by degrees. "Do you want some help?"

"If I have to go in there alone tonight, and I'm not back out by morning, call Hawk. He'll know what to do."

Lee's back was up. "Betty is one of our own . . ."

"I know, but Kangting has got an army out there. I want to keep the casualties to a minimum."

"Yes, sir."

Carter patted him on the arm. "It'll work out, Lee. I promise you."

Lee nodded. "Okay, sir."

Carter reached Colonel Trat at his home, and the man agreed to meet at his office downtown in twenty minutes.

A couple of Lee's technicians were checking the car Betty had used to come in from the country house. They hadn't found a thing.

"No signs of a struggle, sir," one of them said. "She just parked the car, locked up, and disappeared."

Even at that hour there was traffic along Rama Street. Betty had parked there and had been taken. But why had she parked out front, and not around back where the other

AXE staffers parked? It didn't make sense, unless she had seen something and had gotten out to investigate. Too many holes, he thought.

He drove over to Colonel Trat's office and went up the back way, as before, arriving just a minute after the policeman.

"Kangting has kidnapped a friend of mine," Carter said without preamble.

"Who?"

"Betty Chi Doi-ko."

Colonel Trat's eyes narrowed. He knew the name. "Amalgamated Press?"

"I knew her from a few years ago. We had dinner together tonight. She had to stop by her office, but she never made it. They found her car parked out front."

"And that means she was kidnapped? By Robert Kangting?"

"Yes."

"Explain this to me please, Mr. Carson," Trat said, a dangerous glint in his eyes, his lips compressed.

"She was researching a story on him. She was sharing her notes with me. She was probably seen with me."

"I see," Trat said. "And what is it, exactly, that you wish me to do?"

"I'm reporting a missing person," Carter snapped. "I want you to go out to Kangting's compound and investigate."

"On the basis of what, exactly?"

Carter took a deep breath and counted to ten. He could understand Trat's position. Kangting was a highly respected Thai national, and Carter was nothing more than a meddlesome American cop with some sort of a grudge against the Chinese. It was a bad business no matter how you looked at it.

"Will you investigate?"

Trat hesitated for a beat, but then he nodded. "Yes, of course I will investigate. A missing person. Here in

Bangkok. A respected member of the fourth estate. Of course. In the morning my people will get on it.''

"Thank you," Carter said, careful to keep his tone neutral. He started to turn to go, but Colonel Trat stopped him.

"Mr. Carson, it would be most unfortunate should you go barging out to Mr. Kangting's home to bother him. Most unfortunate indeed. Despite your status here, Thailand is a nation of laws and justice. The criminal element—any criminal element—will be dealt with. Do you take my meaning?''

"I do," Carter said. "But take my meaning, Colonel. If it is discovered that Robert Kangting has indeed been involved in the murders of American citizens, and has been involved in the kidnapping of Miss Doi-ko, he will be brought to justice no matter his financial status.''

"I couldn't agree with you more, Mr. Carson.''

At a pay phone in the lobby of the Indra Hotel on Raj Damri Road, Carter dialed the number Bob Mills had given him. It was answered on the third ring by Mills himself.

"This is Carter.''

"What's up?" Mills asked.

"I may need you and your people after all.''

"I'm listening.''

"A friend of mine may have been kidnapped this evening by Robert Kangting.''

"How about the local constabulary? Any help?''

"Not without positive evidence.''

"Which, I suspect, you are going after now," Mills said.

"If you don't hear from me by morning, Kangting's people will have me. You can go from there.''

"I suppose I'll be getting a call from Washington.''

"It's likely.''

"What about right now, Carter? Do you want me to tag along?''

"Not yet. I'm just covering my ass.''

Mills hesitated a moment. "Are you up to it, Carter?''

"We'll see, won't we.''

Mills hesitated again before answering. "We'll be there for you, Carter. And good luck."

"Thanks," Carter said, and he hung up. He went back out to his Mercedes.

He unholstered his Luger, levered a round into the firing chamber, and checked the safety. He didn't bother with the silencer. He didn't care if it made noise. In fact he wanted to make a lot of noise.

He laid the gun down on the seat beside him, put the car in gear, and pulled away from the curb. He headed across the railroad tracks, past the Victory Monument, and out on the highway toward the airport, his adrenaline beginning to pump again.

Carter cruised past the entrance to Kangting's compound, watching it in the rearview mirror. The front gate was lit, and he could see the loom of lights back in the jungle, along the fence line, he presumed. He had seen no movement of any kind, nor had he seen the van that Don Tak, the AXE surveillance man, was supposed to be working out of.

A couple of blocks away, he pulled over and parked, dousing the lights and shutting off the engine. He left the keys beneath the seat, grabbed his Luger, and got out of the car.

There were a few other houses on that road. A pair of headlights appeared in the distance. Carter stepped off the road and pushed his way into the jungle. A big truck passed on the highway, its taillights disappearing in the distance.

For a moment, waiting there in the darkness, Carter had a vision of Betty as he had first seen her standing nude in his shower, the curtain held back with one hand, one hip cocked, a grin on her pretty face. And now Kangting had her.

He headed through the thick jungle growth, keeping parallel and about twenty yards in from the road until he came to the corner of Kangting's compound, the fence angling back into the jungle.

Crouching down in the brush, he could see the lights atop

the tall fence every fifty yards or so. He also spotted at least two closed-circuit television cameras, up high on stanchions, looking outward along a no-man's-land cleared of the lush undergrowth.

Kangting valued his privacy. This was more like a fortress than a home.

Carter followed the clearing along the fence line for a hundred yards or so back into the jungle. He stopped just opposite one of the lights and television cameras. He got down on one knee, and holding his Luger in both hands, he took aim at the camera, squeezed off a shot, sparks flying from the monitor, then switched aim to the light and put it out.

Holstering his Luger on the run, Carter jumped up, emerged from the jungle, crossed the now dark no-man's-land, and scrambled up the fence, heaving himself over the top and down the other side.

He hit the ground hard, rolled once, then jumped up and within a half-dozen steps reached the protective darkness of the jungle. He was now within Kangting's compound, and the man—or at least his staff—knew that they had an intruder on their hands.

Carter shoved his way through the dense undergrowth, working his way farther into the compound at right angles to the fence line. The big house was somewhere within. At best, he figured, Kangting would have a few dozen guards in residence. With any luck they would get in each other's way in the darkness. They were pros, but just how disciplined they were was anyone's guess. He'd find that out tonight.

There were no sounds of any alarm. No lights. No sirens. No baying dogs or shouting search parties. Nothing. Just silence.

In ten minutes Carter had reached the edge of the clearing in which Kangting's palatial home and the other buildings were located.

The clearing was lit, but the house was mostly in darkness.

Two cars were parked outside—one of Kangting's Rollses and Elizabeth's Ferrari—but there was no movement. And not a guard in sight.

It wasn't right. The fence was monitored. The fact that one of the television cameras had gone down would have shown up on someone's alarm board. Yet no one had come out to check. Nor had anyone come to investigate the two gunshots.

Carter circled around to the back of the big house before he stepped out from the jungle. He hesitated for only a moment, then, keeping low and zigzagging across the expansive lawn, raced for the veranda.

Halfway across, the rear lawn was suddenly bathed in lights, as bright as if it were day.

Carter pulled up short, raising his Luger.

"Put down your weapon, Mr. Carter," an amplified voice boomed from the house.

In unison, a dozen armed men suddenly appeared at the veranda, another dozen or so on the roof, equally as many to the right, and still another dozen or more to the left, their weapons up and at the ready.

Carter lowered his Luger and looked over his shoulder. At least twenty men lined the edge of the jungle.

"That's right, Mr. Carter," the amplified voice instructed. "Just drop your gun, please, and no one will get hurt tonight."

TEN

The big gate guard Carter had hassled on his first visit to Kangting's compound came down from the veranda and crossed the lawn to where Carter stood. The man had a mean glint in his eyes and his upper lip was curled in disdain. He was unarmed.

Carter had dropped Wilhelmina to the grass and stood flatfooted waiting for the big man to reach him. He knew what was coming, and he was preparing himself for it. He also knew that Kangting probably wouldn't order his death, at least not yet, at least not until he found out just who Carter was and how much Washington already knew or had guessed.

"Just don't kill him," Kangting had probably told his people. "Anything else will be okay."

"We were expecting you," the big man said. He was swarthy. Carter thought he looked North African, possibly Algerian. A big scar ran from his cheek to his forehead over his left eye.

"I didn't come alone."

The big man grinned. "Oh, yes, you did."

"There are others who know I'm here."

"You do not have to lie. All of us are impressed by your feats."

Carter held himself in check. The man had all but admitted Kangting was in league with the Chinese. What other feats could he be talking about? And how did he know about them?

The big man glanced down at Carter's Luger. "Are you carrying any other weapons?"

Carter said nothing.

"We can do this the hard way or the easy way. Any other hardware?"

Carter extended his arms away from his body, inviting a search. If the big man was wary, he didn't show it. He approached Carter and patted him down. As he was bent over, Carter suddenly clenched both hands together, making one large fist, and brought them down on the base of the man's neck.

The big man staggered and went down on one knee. Carter stepped back as the troops surrounding him raised their weapons, the noise audible even at a distance.

"*Merde*," the big man swore in French. He got heavily to his feet, looked into Carter's eyes for a few long seconds, and then without warning doubled up his fist and smashed it into Carter's chest, knocking him backward, taking his breath away.

Carter pulled himself together and straightened up. He smiled. "One-on-one, scum," he said softly in gutter French. "Just you and me."

Surprise flickered in the man's eyes. He nodded. "That would give me a great deal of pleasure, monsieur. But later. For the moment you are an honored guest."

"Any time."

The big man motioned for one of the other guards to come down from the house. The guard came across the lawn, locked and loaded his M-16, and placed the muzzle against the base of Carter's head.

"Now, let us try this again," the big man said. Quickly and efficiently he patted Carter down, this time coming up with the extra clip of ammunition for Wilhelmina and the silencer, which he pocketed. He missed the stiletto.

When he was finished, he and the other guard stepped back a respectful distance and motioned toward the house. Carter took his time lowering his arms and straightening his jacket before he preceded them across the lawn, up to the veranda, and into the back of the house.

They walked down a short corridor and went through a door into a broad, well-lit room, that turned out to be an exercise room. Betty was nude, her body spread grotesquely across a weight-lifting machine, heavy weights attached by cords to her wrists and ankles, her back arched painfully over a bar. A guard assigned to her was running his hands over her body.

In one fluid motion Carter had his stiletto in his right hand, and he threw it, the razor-sharp blade burying itself to the hilt in the chest of the man whose hands were all over Betty.

The man grunted in surprise, then he toppled backward over the exercise equipment.

The big, French-speaking guard kicked Carter in the small of the back, sending him sprawling on his hands and knees, as the other guards came after him.

Carter rolled over, managing to ward off most of the blows from rifle butts aimed at his head.

"Enough!" the big guard bellowed. "Someone take care of Mercado!"

The men around Carter backed off, and the big guard hauled Carter to his feet. This time when he patted him down he didn't miss an inch.

"No more toys, eh?" he hissed. "My mistake, for which I will pay. But before that happens, let me assure you that you will pay more."

"How about right now, pig?" Carter asked softly.

The big man stiffened a little. But he was a pro. He managed a tight smile. "In due time. I want you angry. I want you not merely to dislike us, but I want you to really hate me. Just as you hated Mercado for a moment.'' He glanced over at Betty, who was watching them with frightened eyes. The gesture was clear to Carter. "Oh, yes, monsieur, you will hate me very much before we are finished here.''

"And then I will kill you," Carter said. "Make no mistake.''

The big man looked just a little less certain than before, but he shoved Carter back.

"He's dead, André," one of the guards said, looking up from the body.

"Strap him down!" the big one called André ordered, indicating Carter. He went over to the fallen man and yanked out the stiletto, wiping the blade on the guard's jacket.

Two guards brought a chair around, shoved Carter into it, and tied his arms and legs together, looping the cords around and beneath the chair. Two others removed the dead man.

"Tell Mr. Kangting we are ready for him," André snapped. He came over to where Carter was sitting, looked down at him contemptuously, then roughly hauled him around so that he was directly in front of Betty.

"Are you all right?" Carter asked her. He could see the fear and pain in her eyes.

She managed to nod her head slightly. "Sorry to get you into this, Nick," she rasped.

"Help is on its way."

She smiled.

"Touching," André said. He bent down over Carter and brought the tip of the stiletto up so that it was a quarter of an inch from Carter's right eye. "I am wondering how well you would do with only one eye?"

"Frightened little men need to even the odds," Carter said without flinching or trying to move his face away from the blade.

André's nostrils flared. He flicked the blade a little lower, opening a two-inch cut high on Carter's right cheek. Blood began to flow immediately. Still Carter did not move a muscle.

"Why don't you cut my ropes? Just you and me, André. Send the others away. We can work it out."

Betty was watching them, her eyes wide. Carter winked at her. She took a deep breath and let it out slowly.

"Admirable," Robert Kangting said from the doorway. "Very admirable indeed, Mr. Carter."

André straightened up and turned around. "He killed Mercado with this," he said.

Kangting came across the gym, glanced at the knife in André's hand, and at the cut beneath Carter's eye. "What did you expect the man to do, lie down meekly and take whatever came his way?"

André said nothing. The other guards had backed away respectfully.

Kangting pressed his fingertips to the blood on Carter's cheek, then raised his hand so that he could look at it. "Amazing, the differences in blood," he said softly. "From this man, it comes from an extraordinarily strong heart. It flows through a body well used to pain and stress." He took a handkerchief from the pocket of his silk robe and delicately wiped his fingers clean. "This man cannot be broken, André. Don't you see it in his eyes? He could be beaten, tortured, drugged, and yet he would still have some inner reserve from which he could draw more energy than you could imagine was humanly possible."

The big man did not know what to say.

Kangting gently drew André aside. "Listen to me, André. We are in the presence of the ultimate professional, a killing machine, if you will, able to withstand anything thrown his way." Kangting smiled.

"Sir?" André asked.

"Almost anything," Kangting said. He took the stiletto.

Carter suddenly knew what was coming, and he could see from Betty's eyes that she knew as well. It was what they had been trained for. In AXE you understood the risks you were taking in the field. You understood what could happen. And you had accepted, as part of the job, a willingness to deal with whatever came. But Kangting was correct: this now would be nearly impossible for Carter to bear, and the Killmaster did not know if he could stand up to it.

"Yes, Mr. Carter, I can see that you do understand," Kangting said. He looked at Betty's spread-eagled body for a long time before he turned back.

"What do you want, Kangting?" Carter asked.

"What is your name?"

"Nick Carter."

Kangting nodded, and smiled slightly. "There, you see, André? We are making some progress after all." He turned back to Carter. "Who are your employers, Mr. Nick Carter?"

Carter hesitated for just a moment. He glanced at Betty, then at the stiletto in Kangting's hand, and he sagged a little in his chair. "The U.S. State Department."

"Yes?"

"Special Investigations Branch."

"What were you doing in Bangkok?"

"Investigating the murders of Gordon Guthrie and Carlton Reed."

"But they were CIA officers, from what I've read," Kangting said. "Why is the State Department involved?"

Again Carter hesitated, but when Kangting glanced over at Betty, he blurted his answer. "They suspected that your people killed them."

"Oh?" Kangting said. "Why?"

"We didn't know . . ."

Kangting whirled on Betty, bringing the knife up.

"I swear it!" Carter shouted.

Kangting held the blade inches from Betty's breasts.

"I swear to God! Someone saw Guthrie and Reed near here, and a few hours later they were dead. My government contacted your government, but they got the runaround. It was me outside on the ledge at the Thai embassy in Washington that night.''

Kangting turned back, definitely interested now. ''And what was it that you heard up there?''

''Nothing,'' Carter said, shaking his head.

Kangting's lips compressed.

''Nothing. I heard someone talking inside. But then the window opened and the guards below spotted me and opened fire.''

''How did you escape? How did you get downstairs?''

''Your daughter helped me,'' Carter said, and Kangting's eyes widened a little. Carter had scored at least one point. ''I came through her bedroom window, I told her someone was trying to kill me.''

''And when I came to the door?''

''I was hiding in her bathroom.''

Kangting shook his head. ''I don't think I believe you . . .''

''Ask her, Mr. Kangting. Then when I came here to Bangkok, she and I went out to dinner and dancing. Afterward we went to my room in the hotel where we made love. Ask her. It's true.''

''Lies!'' Kangting bellowed. The guards, including André, all stepped back a pace.

''Ask her! I'm not lying. I can describe her body for you if you want.''

Kangting was shaking with rage, his knuckles white on the stiletto's hilt.

''She told me what the Chinese have offered you,'' Carter said into the silence of the room.

Kangting stepped back almost as if he had received a physical blow.

''Captain Chomo confirmed it on the lake before I killed him.''

''And you have transmitted this belief to your government?'' Kangting demanded.

Carter forced himself to hesitate for only a split second, as if he were a man about to be caught in a lie. "Before I came out here I telexed everything to my boss in Washington. They know everything. They know I am here, and help is on its way."

"I wonder," Kangting said, regaining his control.

Time was all he had at this point, Carter thought. If he could stall them until morning, Mills would be coming in with his people. Even if they weren't successful, they'd make enough noise so that Colonel Trat would have to do something.

"It's Hong Kong," Carter said. "We know all about it."

This time Kangting's reaction was not what Carter expected. The man seemed genuinely surprised. Almost puzzled. "Hong Kong?" he asked.

"Yes," Carter said. "The Chinese are taking over in 1997. They've offered its administration to you."

Kangting smiled. "Hong Kong," he said. "Intriguing. But have you any idea how old I would be in 1997, Mr. Carter?"

Carter said nothing. He had the feeling, though, that he had somehow missed the mark. If not Hong Kong, then what? What was it the Chinese had offered him?

"No, Mr. Carter, I have no interest in Hong Kong. So you see it does not matter what you have transmitted to your government, if indeed you have transmitted anything— which I sincerely doubt you have—because it is not true."

He turned abruptly and went to Betty.

"I'm telling you the truth!" Carter shouted.

Kangting reached up with his free hand and caressed Betty's cheek. He let his fingers trace a light path down her throat to her left breast, where he lingered a moment at the nipple. He sighed deeply and turned back. "Such a pretty woman. Such a handsome, strong man." He shook his head, and handed the stiletto back to André.

"There are others who will come looking for me," Carter said.

Kangting ignored him. "I'll be leaving within a few hours, André."

"What about these two?"

"Kill them," Kangting said.

"Yes, sir."

"But wait until I am out of the city, please. I will send word."

"Of course," André said.

Kangting took a long last look at Betty, then at Carter, and turned on his heel and left the big room, the door closing behind him hard, the noise like a pistol shot.

For a second or two André's eyes were locked into Carter's. "Is it true? Did you make love with Elizabeth?"

"If we're to be killed in the morning, how about something to eat and drink? And how about some clothes for the woman?"

André stepped in close. "Did you make love with Elizabeth?"

The man was in love with her, Carter realized. "Yeah," he said with a leering grin. "And let me tell you, André, she was a lousy lay . . ."

André smashed a fist into Carter's face, knocking him over backward, his head bouncing on the floor, stars exploding before his eyes.

From a distance he could feel himself being lifted upright and put back in place in front of Betty's spread-eagled body. André had moved off. Carter heard his voice from behind.

"You have two hours," André was saying. "Enjoy the slut, but don't kill her, and make sure Carter sees everything!"

"André!" Carter roused himself enough to shout. But he heard the door slam. "André!"

A dozen guards all crowded around, shedding their weapons and their jackets, laughing and joking roughly.

"You bastards!" Carter shouted.

One of them slapped him hard in the face, nearly knocking him over again. Another whipped out a knife and began cutting the ropes that held Betty to the weight machine.

A couple of the guards spread an exercise mat out on the floor. They dragged Carter and his chair to the head of the mat. "Let's give him a ringside seat!" someone said, and the others laughed.

They'd cut Betty down and dragged her, kicking and screaming, over to the mat. At the last moment she managed to break free. She swiveled on her heel and drove a knee hard into the crotch of one of the guards. The man doubled over in pain, the air whooshing out of his lungs. One of the others grabbed her by the hair and yanked her roughly around. She raked his face with her long nails, opening up four long gashes in his cheek, and he reeled backward.

But the others were on her then, one of them landing a right hook to her chin. Her head snapped back, and she crumpled unconscious to the floor.

"The bitch," spat the guard whose face she'd laid open, kicking her in the ribs. The others shoved him aside and dragged her body to the mat.

"Me first," the man with the bloody face said, standing over her and unzipping his trousers. "I'll teach you, you—"

"Stop!" a woman shouted from the doorway at the far end of the room.

Everyone looked up as Elizabeth Kangting strode into the gym. She was shaking, and white with rage.

"You don't belong here, Miss Kangting," one of the men said. "Your father—"

Elizabeth came up to him and slapped him in the face, the slap loud in the suddenly quiet room. She looked at the others one at a time, her lips compressed, her eyes narrowed.

"Take your weapons and get out of here! Now! All of you!"

"We cannot do that, miss," the one with the bleeding cheek said.

In three steps Elizabeth had reached one of the M-16s. She grabbed it, cycled the ejector slide, and expertly pointed the weapon at him. "Five . . . four . . . three . . . . two . . ."

The guard scrambled backward, away from the mat.

"Get out of here! Take your weapons and leave, or I shall have to call my father back, and you will not like what I have to say to him!" She raised the gun a little higher. "Animals!" she spat.

"We cannot, Miss Kangting," one of the guards said, his hands spread. "They are supposed to die in the morning."

"And so they shall," Elizabeth said. "As soon as my father leaves. I'll kill them myself if need be. But in the meantime they will not be mistreated. This woman is not yours to play with!"

"But André . . ."

"I will deal with André. For the moment you must decide if you wish to deal with me, and ultimately with my father."

It was enough for the guards. They began gathering their weapons and clothing and leaving the gym. Elizabeth lowered the gun. "I'll just keep this," she said. "I don't trust either of them."

"We'll be outside," one of the guards said, and they all left, closing the door behind them.

Elizabeth glanced down at Betty, whose eyes were fluttering. She was moaning in pain. "Bitch," Elizabeth said.

"It's not her fault," Carter said.

Elizabeth looked at him, and then walked over. "No, I don't suspect it is. It's been you, hasn't it, from the moment you came through my window in Washington. I should have had you killed then."

"Why didn't you?"

She looked at him closely, as if she were trying to see through him, trying to divine some secret. "You looked . . . interesting to me at the time."

"I was doing my job," he said. "And at least I don't kill innocent people."

"There are no innocent people," she snapped. "Now my father is displeased with me. I have lost face in his eyes. You can't know what that means . . ."

"What about us?"

"You will die as my father ordered, the moment he leaves. And I shall kill you with my own hands."

"Why?"

"You used me! I protected you, and you used me!"

"Only because I had to, Elizabeth. Were the circumstances different—"

"Don't lie to me!" she shrieked.

"Your father is working with the Chinese Communists. Did you know that?"

"Yes, and so am I," Elizabeth said. She stepped a little closer, raised the M-16 to Carter's head, and snapped the safety to the off position.

"Why?"

"You'll never know, Nick Carter," she said, pressing the barrel against his temple. "Captain Chomo was my fianceé. So, you see, you are going to die this morning for a reason you did not suspect. Maybe I won't even wait until my father leaves. Maybe now is as good a time as any . . ."

ELEVEN

Betty got up slowly and soundlessly from the mat. Carter could see her out of the corner of his eye.

He looked up into Elizabeth's eyes. "One last thing," he said softly. Her finger was turning white on the M-16's trigger.

She just looked at him.

"Kiss me."

"What?"

"First kiss me," he said. It was her vanity. Betty had called her the spider woman. Elizabeth had to believe that she was irresistible to men. Even to a man she was about to kill.

Her expression softened a little. She moved the barrel of the M-16 away from Carter's temple and started to bend toward him, when Betty came at her.

Elizabeth felt or heard something over her shoulder, because she suddenly straightened up and spun around, bringing up the M-16. Betty reached her at the last possible moment, batting the gun barrel aside with one hand while snapping a karate chop to Elizabeth's collarbone with the other.

Elizabeth shrieked in pain, the rifle clattering to the floor.

"Leave her alone, Elizabeth!" Carter shouted hoarsely for the benefit of the guards who might be listening just outside the door.

Betty shoved the rifle aside with her foot as she charged, but Elizabeth was just as quick on her feet, sidestepping and lashing out with her long, finely manicured fingernails, raking Betty across the neck as she passed.

Both women turned toward each other and then stopped, each taking the measure of the other for the moment. Carter was struggling with his bonds, but there was little he could do. It would take hours to get free. Hours they did not have. It would be up to Betty now.

"You won't get out of here alive," Elizabeth gasped panting.

"One of us won't, Miss Kangting," Betty said, her voice low. She feinted left, but Elizabeth followed her, and they stopped again.

"Elizabeth?" Carter said.

Elizabeth did not take her eyes off Betty's. "What?"

"Step aside. Let us get out of here. When it's over we'll do our best to keep you out of it."

"You fool," she hissed, and she suddenly charged.

Betty was ready for her. This time she sidestepped, shoving Elizabeth off-balance with a left jab, and then smashing a roundhouse right into her jaw. Elizabeth's head went back and she went to one knee, but she rolled left as Betty kicked out, and she jumped lightly to her feet, her white skirt hiked up to her hips.

She was five feet from the M-16. She turned and dived toward it. Betty was on her in four steps, both women's hands now curled around the weapon. Then they were rolling over and over, the gun between them.

Betty jammed the heel of her free hand under Elizabeth's chin and began pushing backward, forcing Elizabeth's head back, the muscles in her arm and shoulder rippling as she put every ounce of her strength into it.

Elizabeth had the leverage suddenly with the rifle, and she shoved it up so that the barrel was pressed against Betty's throat. She began working her fingers down the stock toward the trigger guard, her legs tight around Betty's waist, preventing her from moving.

Realizing what was happening, Betty reared back, clamping her fingers around Elizabeth's throat and smashing her head against the floor. Once. A second time. A third time. Each blow diminished Elizabeth's strength, until finally her eyes fluttered, and she let go of the rifle and slumped back on the floor.

Betty took Elizabeth's throat in both hands and began to deliberately squeeze the life out of her.

"Betty—no!" Carter called out.

Betty hadn't heard him.

"Betty!"

"She's a murderess!" Betty said over her shoulder.

"So will you be if you kill her like this now."

"Goddamnit," Betty swore, thumping Elizabeth's head on the floor, then releasing her throat and scrambling backward, off her.

Elizabeth's purple face began to return to a normal color. She wouldn't be out for long.

Betty got to her feet, came to Carter, and hurriedly undid the cords that held him. When he was free he jumped up and took Betty in his arms.

"Are you all right?" he asked.

"You sure as hell showed up in the nick of time," she said dryly.

"Your car was in front of the hotel. Why?"

"When I drove past I saw Don Tak sitting alone in the front seat of a car. When I went back to talk to him, a half dozen of Kangting's people showed up out of nowhere and grabbed me."

"What did they do with Tak?"

"He was already dead," she said.

Carter gave her his coat. "Tie her up," he said, indicating

Elizabeth. "And gag her. We're getting out of here."

As Betty was doing it, Carter grabbed the M-16, checked the load and safety, and hurried across to the door through which Kangting had gone. He listened for a moment, then glanced back and watched until Betty was finished.

When she jumped up, Carter eased the door open and looked out. A short corridor opened onto a dressing room with floor-to-ceiling mirrors. No one was in sight.

Betty joined him, and together they slipped out of the exercise room, closing and locking the door behind them. They moved down the corridor, through the dressing room, and through a narrow alcove into another corridor that seemed to run the width of the house, front to back. Somewhere toward the front they could hear music and someone talking in low tones. Kangting was getting ready to leave sometime that morning, but there wasn't much of a chance of stopping him. Not alone, with only one weapon between them.

Carter turned right, toward the rear of the house, Betty directly behind him. They went through the open door into the big kitchen, empty at this hour of the morning, then found a door leading to a narrow loading dock outside.

The night was warm and very humid. They could hear the night birds and insects back in the jungle, and smell the odors of night-blooming flowers and the fetid smells of the open canal.

Carter helped Betty down from the loading dock, and they hurried along the length of the house to the far corner where they waited for a moment as Carter just eased to the edge and looked around.

There were lights but no movement. Kangting's Rolls-Royce and Elizabeth's Ferrari were parked in the front. He didn't think Betty would have the strength to make it back through the jungle, over the fence, and up to the road to his car. And he seriously doubted if he would make it either. Their only way out now was the Rolls or the Ferrari.

Carter motioned for Betty to move out, and they slipped around the corner and hurried to the front of the house, where they stopped at the side of the entry veranda.

Kangting himself was out front talking with several of his guards, among them the big one called André. Two other men, M-16s slung over their shoulders, stood next to the Rolls. Every now and then they glanced up at the sky to the north, as if waiting for something to appear. A helicopter, Carter figured. It wouldn't be long now before Kangting would be heading out.

Suddenly lights came on all over the compound, and a siren began shrieking. The guards had evidently gone into the exercise room and sounded the alarm.

Kangting and the others looked up, then hurried across the veranda and into the house. The two by the car had come to attention and brought their weapons to the ready.

It was now or never, Carter thought. Either the keys were in one of the cars, or they were not. But they had just run out of options.

Carter jumped up and raced around the edge of the veranda. He'd made ten yards before the guards by the car realized what was going on, and they spun around.

He fired two short bursts, catching both men in the chest before they had a chance to fire, driving the guards backward into the fender of the Rolls.

They reached the cars three seconds later, Carter checking the Rolls, Betty the Ferrari.

"Here!" Betty called, hauling open the Ferrari's passenger side door.

A guard came out the front door of the house. Carter snapped off a burst, hitting the man in the neck, then he ran back to the Ferrari. He tossed the M-16 over the top of the car to Betty and climbed in behind the wheel as she fired a long burst, raking the front of the house.

Carter started the car, jammed it in gear, and Betty tossed the gun aside, climbed in, and even before she had her door

closed he popped the clutch and jammed the accelerator to
the floor.

The powerful engine spun them around, spitting a
hundred-foot rooster tail of sand and gravel up over the
veranda, and they were screaming down the circular driveway to the road that led through the jungle to the gate.

"Hang on!" Carter shouted as he hit second gear with a
racing change, and they surged forward.

A few shots from the house shattered the rear window,
but then they were accelerating down the narrow jungle
road. Carter slammed the Ferrari into third, and when the
gate appeared they were already doing in excess of eighty
and still picking up speed.

Two of Kangting's men charged out of the guardhouse,
ran into the middle of the road, and started to raise their
weapons. Before they had a chance to fire, however, they
realized there wasn't enough time and leaped out of the way.

Carter had the car up to nine thousand RPM when he
shifted into fourth and they hit the big gate, crashing through
it like a hot knife through butter, the hood ripping off, and
the windshield starring.

At the road he had to heel-and-toe the brake and gas pedal
as he slammed the car back into third, and soon they were
out on the highway.

The Ferrari's tail gave a little wiggle as he floored the
pedal and they screamed down the highway into the night
back toward Bangkok, passing a hundred miles per hour
and still accelerating before they'd reached the edge of
Kangting's property.

The half-hour drive took them something under ten minutes. Carter didn't bother looking down at the speedometer,
but he figured they had to be doing 150 miles per hour along
some stretches, oil blowing back from the open engine so
that when they finally reached Bangkok, he could barely
see out the windshield.

He spotted a telephone booth and turned the car off the road, coming to a screeching halt.

"Where'd you learn to drive?" Betty asked as he jumped out.

"Indianapolis," he yelled over his shoulder. Carter dialed the number Mills had given him. The CIA troubleshooter answered on the first ring.

"Yeah?"

"It's me. Right now. Kangting's compound. At least five dozen armed men. Automatic weapons at least. Kangting will be moving out shortly. I'm calling out the Thai police. Watch yourself."

"Right," Mills said.

Carter broke the connection, and then dialed Trat's home. There was no answer after four rings. Carter hung up and dialed Trat's office. The colonel answered on the first ring.

"Carson. I've just escaped from Kangting's house. He tried to kill me and Miss Doi-ko. Lots of men, lots of automatic weapons. Are you going to help this time?"

Carter could hear someone in the background, and what sounded like a communications radio.

"Where are you, Mr. Carson?"

"Are you going to help, or do I have to call Washington?"

"We already are in communication with Washington," Trat said. "There has been a report of gunfire from Mr. Kangting's compound."

"That's right. And he'll be leaving it at any moment. Probably by helicopter."

"I will alert the airport. He will not leave with his airplane. You do have our cooperation, Mr. Carson."

"You'd better alert the port authority. He might try to reach his yacht."

"That too," Trat said.

"We're in town, near the railroad tracks. A half a block from the Suan Pakkard Palace. Red Ferrari. We'll wait for you."

"My people are on their way, Mr. Carson. But from this moment on, this is a matter for my government. Do I make myself perfectly clear?"

"Just hurry!" Carter said. He crashed the telephone down and stepped out of the booth. Betty had climbed out of the car.

"What next?" she asked.

"Trat's people are on their way, along with Bob Mills and his crew. We're to wait for them here. You'd better call the office and tell them you're safe. Have them call Hawk."

They'd left him his cigarettes. While he waited for Betty to finish on the phone he lit one, and made a quick search of Elizabeth's car. He found nothing of significance in the glove compartment or trunk, but in a door panel map compartment he found a map of northern Thailand showing the borders with Burma and Laos. It was curious, he thought, that Elizabeth would have such a map and not one of Bangkok where she lived, unless she had driven up there recently . . . .

The first of the sirens sounded in the distance as Betty stepped out of the phone booth. She seemed even more shaken than before.

"What is it, Betty?"

"They found Charlie Knell."

"Dead?"

She nodded, plucking the cigarette from Carter's fingers and taking a deep drag. "Shot to death in the back of the head. Another execution. Makes four from my office alone."

"It's all over now," Carter said.

She looked up at him and shook her head. "I don't think so, Nick. Not quite yet. We're not going to get there in time to stop him. I'm sure he's gone already."

Carter nodded. "And he won't be able to come back to Thailand."

"Maybe he hadn't intended on coming back. Maybe we

caught him just before he left.''

"We'll find him, Betty."

Colonel Trat and Bob Mills arrived nearly at the same time, along with a contingent of at least two hundred Bangkok police and Thai soldiers. Carter and Betty climbed into Trat's car, and they screamed down the road back toward Kangting's compound.

"We have two army helicopters coming in for support," Trat explained. "The airport has been sealed as has the river and the port. We're also watching the train station and all the highways out of town."

Trat's aide sat in the front with the driver. He answered a steady stream of radio communications from the units behind them in convoy as well as the units now spreading throughout the city.

"The choppers are on their way, sir," he said over his shoulder.

"Very good. Have them watch for any air traffic near the Kangting property. Challenge and if necessary follow, but under no circumstances are they to fire unless I give the order, or unless they are fired upon."

"Yes, sir," the aide said, and he turned back to his radio.

"There will be bloodshed enough this morning, I am thinking, without adding unnecessary loss of lives," Colonel Trat said, then he turned to Betty. "May I ask, Miss Doi-ko, what you were doing last evening—or should I say this morning—at Mr. Kangting's home?"

"I was on my way to my office, when I was kidnapped right off the street in front of the Intercontinental."

"Just like that?"

"I saw one of my reporters sitting in a car. When I stopped to talk to him, Kangting's men came out of the darkness and took me."

"And what of this reporter? Mr. . . . ?"

"Don Tak. He is dead, Colonel, shot in the back of the head. Along with another of my reporters, Charlie Knell.

Also shot dead through the back of the head. And I was very nearly raped and killed, as was my friend Mr. Carson very nearly killed.''

Colonel Trat shook his head and digested this information for a moment or two. "And you, Mr. Carson, what was it you were doing visiting Mr. Kangting in the middle of the night?"

"Miss Doi-ko and I were together for the evening. When she failed to show up at her office, they telephoned me to see if she had already left. I knew what had happened."

Colonel Trat nodded sagely. "Many questions left unanswered. But for now these are serious charges that require serious measures."

Kangting's compound was in darkness when they arrived. Trat's driver pulled up on the highway, and Trat deployed some of his troops around the perimeter, while the others followed him down the dirt road to the gate that Carter had knocked off its hinges.

"I saw at least sixty guards, all of them armed with M-16s," Carter said.

They stopped twenty-five yards in from the gate as they heard the first of the firing coming from the perimeter on the north. Betty remained behind with Trat's driver and two police guards, as Carter borrowed a Colt .45 automatic from one of the soldiers and along with Mills's people hurried on foot the rest of the way into the compound.

The firing intensified to the north as they kept in the darker shadows, watching to the left and right as well as straight ahead. Colonel Trat was somewhere behind them in walkie-talkie communications with the remainder of his people. Overhead they could hear the two army helicopters somewhere to the south, coming in low and fast.

Carter motioned for them to hold up just at the edge of the clearing across which was the main house, dark now like the rest of the compound. They saw two men running across the veranda and then disappearing around back.

Kangting's Rolls was still parked in front, the two guards Carter had shot still lying where they had fallen.

Mills had brought his four field men with him. They seemed capable enough and were armed with Uzi submachine guns.

"Bob and I will take the front doors," Carter said. "I want two of you around the main house to the left, the other two around to the right. We'll meet up in the back. There is a loading dock. But watch yourself, and watch out for us."

They all nodded, checked their weapons, and then on signal, sprinted across the lawn, splitting left and right at the circular driveway.

Mills and Carter held up for a moment behind the Rolls until the other four had disappeared. Carter stuffed the .45 in his belt and picked up the M-16 from one of the fallen guards.

"Watch yourself," he said to Mills, and they hurried around the big car, up onto the veranda, and across to the open front door. They took up positions on either side of the entrance.

Carter was in first, diving low and to the left. Someone fired from across the living room, and Carter snapped off a short burst toward the muzzle flash. A man cried out in pain, then was still.

A second later Mills dived through the doorway, rolling right, firing at a movement down the long corridor.

They lay there in the darkness for a few seconds, listening to the sounds of fighting still off to the north in the jungle and letting their eyes adjust to the lack of light.

"Now!" Carter said softly, and he jumped up, raking the far wall and corridor with fire as he sprinted to the corner around which was the hallway back to the exercise room and bedrooms.

There was no answering fire, and a couple of seconds later Mills jumped up and raced to the opposite side of the corridor opening.

Carter had to admire Mills's abilities. It was obvious he

was not only well trained, but had seen combat at some time in his past.

They leapfrogged their way down the long corridor, stopping to kick open doors, rake the rooms with fire, and then move on, only one of them at any moment on point and therefore exposed to return fire.

But there was no one else in the house. Nor was there anyone in the exercise room where Betty had been held and nearly raped, and where she had almost killed Elizabeth Kangting.

A short burst of automatic weapons fire came from the rear of the house, but then the night was suddenly, ominously silent, except for the helicopters now just off to the north.

"Mr. Mills," one of the CIA field men called from the loading dock.

"In here," Mills said. "Everything okay?"

"There was only one of them, sir. He's dead," the man shouted. "Everything secured in there?"

"Yes," Mills said. "Come on through."

Colonel Trat arrived five minutes later, and then his driver showed up with the police guards and Betty. As far as they could tell, Kangting had left with his daughter and a large contingent of troops, leaving behind about two dozen men, all of whom were now dead or seriously wounded.

The sun was just coming up as they were finishing their initial search, and Trat brought Carter his stiletto and Wilhelmina with its silencer and extra clips of ammunition.

But it wasn't until well after ten before a thorough search of the house and grounds was completed, with absolutely no results.

They were outside at the cars. Someone had brought the Mercedes Carter had driven from the country house to Bangkok the previous evening.

"There is nothing here, Mr. Carson, to indicate that Robert Kangting was anything but what he purported himself to be," Colonel Trat said tiredly. "There will be trouble, of course."

"What about Kangting?"

"He has disappeared."

"His airplane . . . ?"

"And yacht are still in place. He is gone. And now there is a very large mess for me to clean up. A very large mess indeed. I suggest that you leave this country now, Mr. Carson. For good. I can say with assurance that you are no longer welcome in Thailand."

TWELVE

It was nearly noon by the time the doctor checked Betty and stitched the cut in Carter's cheek. Then they drove over to her apartment where she showered and dressed.

They were both dead tired, but Carter wanted to clean up a few details before they went back out to her brother-in-law's country house.

Bob Mills was staying at the Hilton near the embassy. They met him there in the dining room a few minutes after two for a late lunch, after first calling to tell the AXE office that everything was fine and that they'd be by later.

Mills seemed cautiously happy. They all had gin and tonics while they waited for their lunch to arrive.

"That was quite a show," he said. "Maybe we can get things back to normal now."

"Kangting is still out there," Carter noted.

Mills shrugged. "He's too visible a man to stay underground for long. They'll find him. Someone will spot him."

"Have you made your report?" Carter asked.

"It went out an hour ago."

"Is my name mentioned?"

"Only where necessary, Nick. It's classified top secret in any event."

143

"Good," Carter said. AXE would have to be protected at all costs. From this point on, though, it would be up to Hawk in Washington to keep their names out of any report that might be seen by too many people. But he was an old hand at doing that.

"Are you leaving Bangkok soon?" Mills asked.

"Tomorrow, probably. I'd like to get some rest."

"And you, Miss Doi-ko?" Mills asked.

She smiled. "This is my home. And I've got a wire service to run."

"I suppose you got a great story out of it."

She shook her head. "Thai censors. It'll take a while to get it all out. But I'll be working on it. Your name won't be mentioned, if you're interested."

"I appreciate that," Mills said. He wasn't buying for a minute that Betty was nothing more than a wire service reporter, but he said nothing.

They all shook hands after lunch. "Can't say it's been a pleasure, Carter," Mills said.

"But it was interesting," Carter finished, smiling.

Mills laughed. "That it was. Next time you're in Washington, look me up. I'll buy you a drink."

"Sounds good," Carter said.

He and Betty left the hotel and took the Mercedes back over to the AXE office behind the Intercontinental, where Thomas Lee and an anxious staff were waiting for them. Betty closeted herself with her number two man, while Carter telephoned Hawk on an encrypted circuit. It was early in the morning there, but Hawk answered on the first ring.

"Sorry to bother you so late, sir, but we're about wrapped up here," Carter said.

"Are you all right?" Hawk asked.

"Yes, sir."

"And Betty Doi-ko?"

"She'll be all right. She's quite a woman."

"Yes, she is. I've just gotten word that Kangting was spotted in Rangoon."

Carter sat up. "Rangoon? Damn!"

"It wasn't confirmed, though. We're trying to nail it down now. What's going on, Nick?"

Carter quickly explained what had happened at Kangting's compound with him and Betty and Elizabeth, and then with Colonel Trat and the Thai authorities. "His plane and yacht haven't left, and all the highways have been blocked."

"He left by helicopter?"

"Most probably. But I'll bet anything that he hasn't crossed any border yet. My guess is that he's still in Thailand."

"Then the Thai authorities will find him and take care of it," Hawk said. "There's nothing further we can do there."

"Yes, sir," Carter said. He was disappointed, and he didn't really know why, except that the assignment had not ended the way he had wanted it to. The Chinese connection with Kangting was still a big question mark. If Kangting wasn't after Hong Kong, what was it? He said as much to Hawk.

"Until he surfaces, there's nothing we can do about it, Nick. You can't go chasing after a will-o'-the-wisp. Kangting can go anywhere in the world he wants to. And that includes China, if you were right about him."

"Yes, sir," Carter said glumly.

"You're tired, Nick. You've gone through a great deal. Get some rest, and then come in. The Thai government is already starting to make serious noises about getting rid of you."

"Yes, sir," Carter said again. "I'll be heading back tomorrow or the next day."

"Where will you be staying?"

Carter told him about the house Betty was using.

"Just watch yourself, Nick. Kangting may be a man who

holds a grudge. He might be sending someone after you. Especially if he's still somewhere in Thailand.''

"I understand.''

Hawk hesitated a moment. There was a great deal of respect and affection between them. He knew how Carter felt. "Not everything ends up in a neat little package.''

"I've been telling myself just that from the start of this one. But I don't think we've heard the last of Robert Kang-ting.''

"Perhaps not. But for the moment we're off the case.''

"Yes, sir,'' Carter said and he hung up. He lit a cigarette and went to the windows that looked down on the beginning of the afternoon rush hour. Betty wasn't finished with Lee yet, and he had a moment to himself. It was a Friday. If he were back in Washington now, he'd probably be thinking about heading out of the city: the Chesapeake Bay to sail, maybe the Virginia countryside for a quiet weekend, or even New York. But today he was in Bangkok and he knew this assignment wasn't over; his gut was telling him that there was more, much more.

Betty came out of her office, said something to Lee, and then crossed to where Carter stood. She touched his arm and he turned to her.

"All set?'' he asked.

She nodded. "You?''

"I could use a cold drink, a hot shower . . . and you.''

She smiled. "In that order?''

"Preferably.''

"Then what are we waiting for?'' she asked, taking his arm.

The car Betty had used had been brought around to the back parking lot. They left it, taking the Mercedes instead, merging with the heavy afternoon traffic, working their way out toward the less crowded highway. They were both exhausted and bruised.

"How are you feeling?'' he asked at one point.

"Sore but okay,'' she said. "I'm fine now, really.''

"I was frightened for you at Kangting's."

"I know, Nick. I could see it in your eyes. It's probably why Hawk doesn't want people like us working together. We set up a vulnerability in each other. If they had gotten around to you, I would have told them anything they wanted to know."

"In the end I probably would have too," Carter admitted. "Hawk couldn't have encouraged you and Tommy, then."

She shook her head. "No. He said we'd end up dead because of our association. Because of our love . . ."

"He was wrong that time . . ."

"No, Nick, he wasn't wrong," she said. A tear slipped down her cheek. "Christ," she said. "Christ, it still hurts after all this time."

Carter reached out with his free hand and touched her cheek with his fingertips. She reached up and took his hand in hers and held it close against her cheek, as if in some small measure contact with him could ease her pain.

They drove the rest of the way out of the city without talking, listening to the music on the radio, trying to sort out the events of the past few days.

Maybe he wouldn't leave tomorrow, Carter thought. Maybe he'd stay through the weekend. Hawk would understand. And as long as he kept out of sight, Colonel Trat wouldn't make too many waves.

It was nearly five o'clock by the time they reached the gate. Betty jumped out, unlocked it, and swung it open so that Carter could drive through, then she closed and relocked it, and got back into the car.

They drove the rest of the way up to the house and parked in front. Everything inside was as they had left it. Carter's half-finished beer and sandwich were still on the tray on the back veranda overlooking the stream, and the few lights were still on.

"How about a bath for two instead of a shower for one?" Betty asked.

"Sounds good to me," Carter said, taking off his jacket and tossing it over the end of the couch.

Betty had slipped out of her shoes. At the door to the master bedroom wing, she looked back. "And I'll take a cognac."

"Just one?"

She grinned. "Hell, bring the whole bottle; we might stay the night." She disappeared in the back, shedding her blouse as she went.

Carter unstrapped his stiletto and Luger and dropped them on the coffee table, then stepped out of his shoes and went across to the stereo system, where he selected a few tapes and turned the music on low.

At the sideboard he found a bottle of good French cognac and a couple of snifters. He could hear the tub running in the background, even over the music and the gentle sounds of the burbling stream outside. It was peaceful here. Quiet. Safe.

He started back toward the bedroom wing but stopped halfway across the living room. He looked back at the coffee table, staring at his weapons. It *was* quiet here, wasn't it. Peaceful. Safe.

We can't escape ourselves, though, can we, he thought. He'd always been a cautious man. The AXE psychologists said his instinct for survival had somehow turned out to be a thousand percent stronger than average. It had kept him alive through countless tough spots.

He went back to the coffee table, put down the cognac and glasses, and unholstered Wilhelmina. He could smell the clean odor of gun oil, and the fainter odor of fired gunpowder. Wilhelmina was an old, trusted friend. He levered a round into the firing chamber, checked to make sure the safety was in the on position, then shoved the gun in his belt, picked up the bottle and snifters, and crossed the living room.

The bedroom was large, with a huge circular bed in the center, up on a platform. A shimmering tent of mosquito

netting moved softly in the evening breeze. The entire back
wall of the big room was open to the stream and to the
flower garden in back. To the right the room led to a large
marble tub already half filled with steaming water pouring
in from four large taps.

Betty was lying back in the tub, her eyes half closed. A
pretty pink flower floated in the water, sailing back and
forth in the currents.

Carter went across to her, and she opened her eyes and
looked up.

"What took you so long?" she asked sleepily.

"Anticipation is half the pleasure of lovemaking," he
said softly. He poured them both a drink and handed her one.

She cradled the snifter in both hands and watched as he
got undressed. She said nothing as he laid his Luger on the
edge of the tub, but her eyes widened slightly when he was
completely disrobed and she saw the scars on his body.

"You've been around," she said languidly.

He lit them both a cigarette, and then stepped into the
very hot, scented water. As he lay back against the built-in
headrest, a very big sigh escaped his lips as he felt his aches
and pains dissolving in the water.

"I couldn't have said it better," Betty said.

They touched glasses.

"Maybe you can stay the weekend?" she said, and they
drank, the cognac excellent.

"If you can put up with me for that long."

She smiled, and then laughed out loud. "Oh, I think we
can manage somehow. I think it's possible."

Carter reached over and kissed her softly on her lips, her
tongue darting against his.

"I think this is just about where we left off the last time,"
she said when they parted.

"Something like that," he said.

She reached up and shut off the water. Now all they could
hear were the gentle sounds of the stream and the music off
in the distance.

Carter lay back again, sipping his drink, feeling the heat of the water pull away everything bad that had happened to him over the past two weeks. The remainder of this evening, and the weekend, stretched before them. It had been a very long time, he decided, since he had felt such a sense of comfort and well-being. Kangting and everything he represented seemed, for the moment, to be very far away. Nothing could touch them here and now. Nothing.

"What happens when you get back to Washington?" she asked after a long time.

"Desk work for a while, I suppose, until another assignment comes up."

"I meant about Kangting."

"I don't know, Betty. It's up to the politicians now, I suspect."

"But that doesn't sit well with you."

"What makes you say that?"

"Come on, Nick, I've been around. Tommy used to say it wasn't over until all the bad guys were dead or prosecuted."

"I don't think it's over," he admitted.

She sat up and looked at him. "That's why the piece in the bathroom?"

He shrugged.

"Bad feeling?"

He thought about that for a moment. But she was right. He did have a bad feeling. Kangting had become a billionaire by not giving up easily. This time he'd apparently done just that. No, he decided, it wasn't over. And he was about to say so when he heard a noise in the living room. Or rather a diminishing of the music, as if someone had passed in front of one of the speakers. Betty had heard it as well because she stiffened, and looked up toward the doorway.

Carter crushed out his cigarette, set down his drink, and grabbed his Luger, thumbing off the safety.

Betty started to say something, but Carter put a finger to his lips and she held off. He motioned toward the dressing room, which was just off the bedroom, and he climbed carefully out of the tub, padding through the bedroom to the living room doorway.

He flattened himself against the wall, Wilhelmina at the ready, as he strained to listen for another sound, anything. But except for the music there was nothing. He glanced over his shoulder. Betty stood watching the veranda, what looked like a small Beretta automatic in her hand, her wet skin shimmering.

If someone was in the living room, they were waiting now, and listening, wondering why the bedroom was suddenly so quiet.

"I'll get us another drink, darling," he suddenly said out loud, and he dived through the doorway, rolling left toward the back of one of the couches.

Someone fired from near the sideboard, the noise shockingly loud in the room. Carter popped up and fired three quick shots, bracketing the sideboard. A man cried out, and another shot smacked into the doorframe just behind Carter, this one from the edge of the veranda.

Carter got the impression of a figure ducking outside, when Betty fired and the man was shoved sideways over the low rail and into the river.

He jumped up and raced across the room in time to see a body floating downstream. A car started up at the front of the house, and Carter could hear tires spinning on the gravel driveway as he raced down the long veranda and around the side of the house, thorns tearing at his bare skin, the rocks sharp on his feet.

He was in time to see the taillights of a car disappearing down the driveway. He dropped into a shooter's stance and fired off four shots in quick succession, the shells ejecting in long arcs. On the last shot there was a large thump, and a huge fireball rose up through the trees. He'd hit the gas tank.

Someone was coming up behind him, and he spun around, aiming Wilhelmina, his finger squeezing the trigger, until at the last instant the figure stopped, and he realized who it was and pulled back.

Betty stopped in her tracks, understanding what had almost happened. For several long beats they stood like that, facing each other, until Carter slowly rose.

Betty let out a little laugh, straightening up. "I think someone doesn't want us to make love, Nick," she said, a slight tremor in her voice.

Carter crossed the lawn to where she stood at the water's edge. He looked into her eyes for a long time, then took the gun from her hand and put it and his down on the lawn. He took her into his arms and pulled her close, kissing her deeply, her long, smooth body pressed against his.

"Oh, Nick," she said breathlessly when they parted. "How about music and champagne and silk sheets . . ."

He silenced her with his lips, and they sank down together on the cool, soft grass, the night warm and humid, their bodies orange and red in the reflected glow from the flames rising farther down the driveway.

"There may be more of them out there," Betty said.

"Probably," Carter replied, kissing her face and her neck, his lips tracing a pattern down her chest to the nipples of her breasts.

"Oh, God," she cried, her knees rising along his flanks.

Carter lingered a long time at her breasts, the nipples hardening under his touch, her pelvis rising, her back arching, her arms holding him tightly.

Amid all the death and destruction there was this, Carter thought at one point, his tongue tracing a delicate pattern on her slightly rounded belly, his hands on her buttocks, pulling her up to him. He buried himself in her, kissing the backs of her knees and the incredible softness of her thighs, her hips rising to meet his every touch.

"Oh, Nick," she cried as he entered her, pushing deeply, her long legs wrapped around his hips, her arms around his neck, and he pulled her to him, lifting her half off the grass, trying to lose himself even more deeply.

They began to move slowly, their rhythm gradually increasing. There was an all-consuming need and hunger in her that Carter could sense in her every movement. It had been a very long time since she had made love, and he could feel that too in her.

They rose higher and higher, drinking of each other's energy and feel and presence.

"Oh, God," she cried again at the very end, and even the birds and insects were quiet as they both soared over the brink together, neither of them wanting to end the final, delicious moment.

THIRTEEN

Thomas Lee and a couple of technicians from the AXE office came out a few minutes before midnight. They were pretty shook up when they arrived. Something had happened; Carter could see it written all over their faces as they got out of their car.

"What happened? Trouble?" Carter asked as they came up on the front veranda.

"Is Betty all right?" Lee asked.

"She's in back changing," Carter said. "What happened to you?"

"It was Phil Barber. He and Stan were going to bring Betty's car back out here. Phil got behind the wheel, turned the key, and the car blew sky-high. We haven't found a piece of his body that weighs more than a pound."

"They were after Betty—or me. It's Kangting's people."

"I should have known, Mr. Carter, after your call about what happened out here."

"Don't do that to yourself, Lee. Just do the best you can and learn from your mistakes. But Kangting has got a big army, and they know what they're doing."

"They're not going to stop at this," Lee said.

"No, they're not. But neither are we."

"I'm sorry, sir, but I talked with Hawk just before coming out here. He wants you back in Washington on the first available plane. Military transport if need be."

"Why?"

"The Thai government wants you out. You have been declared persona non grata."

"Colonel Trat," Carter said.

"Possibly, but I don't think so. And neither does Hawk. He thinks it's Kangting's doing. If he can't kill you, he can at least get rid of you."

Betty came out. She was wearing a pair of slacks and a light shirt. "I thought I heard you out here—" she started to say, but she stopped in mid-sentence when she caught the look on their faces.

"Kangting's people planted a bomb in your car," Carter said.

"Who got hurt?" she asked.

"Phil Barber," Lee said.

"Oh, God. We're going to have to get some help."

"Hawk told me that we're to lay low for the moment," Lee said, "and let the Thai authorities take care of it—at least for now."

"He wants me back in Washington," Carter said, "but I never got the message. By the time Lee got out here we were gone."

"You can't—" Lee started, but Carter cut him off.

"Clean up the mess here. Betty and I will be leaving within the hour."

"Where to?" Betty asked.

"North, up into the mountains."

"I don't see—"

"Kangting hasn't left Thailand," Carter said. He'd finally figured it out. "My guess is that he's holed up in the mountains somewhere along the border. A training camp, I'd suspect, with the help of the Chinese."

"What for?" Lee asked.

"He never intended to leave Thailand. He wants me dead,

or at the very least out of the country, and all of you to lay low. It's Kangting who is putting on the political pressure.''

"But why, Nick? What does he hope to gain with the Chinese here?''

"He's not going to take over Hong Kong. He's planning on taking over Thailand, his home country. Later perhaps all of the Malay Peninsula. He's planning a coup d'état.''

"He'd never get away with it,'' Lee protested.

"He thinks he can,'' Carter said. "It's why he's been traveling to the West so much during the past year or so. He's got the support of a lot of people in our government, as well as in the Thai government. He's got the money and the following. Hell, he practically owns all of Thailand now as it is. If something happened to him and his empire, Thailand would be in serious economic difficulties.''

"Why the Chinese?'' Betty asked.

"Because he can't do it on his own. He needs the troops. Afterward Thailand will become more closely aligned with Communist China than with the West. They've probably already got their trade agreements hammered out. And in 1997, when Hong Kong reverts to the Chinese, they will have such a big foothold in the region that no one would be able to stop them.''

They all stopped a moment to let what he had said sink in.

"Where up north, though?'' Betty asked. "Thailand is a big country.''

"I saw a map in Elizabeth Kangting's car. Up around Ban Pua. The Mae Nam River.''

"The border with Laos,'' Betty mused.

"That's where it all started,'' Carter said. "Kangting had been spotted up there. It was a big mistake on his part, and ever since then he's been trying to cover it up by killing anyone who got in his way. It's also why he went to Washington when he did. To mend some fences, to convince our government, as well as his own government, that he's nothing more than a man dedicated to the peace and stability of the region.''

"What exactly is it you're going to do up there?" Lee asked. "You can't fight an army."

"We can spot the camp if it's there. I'll stay up there, and Betty can come back and tell Hawk. Then the Thai government will have to believe what's happening. They can send help."

"He'll be watching for you," Lee said.

"No doubt."

By one o'clock they'd gathered up a few supplies for Carter from the house, including some food, extra clothing for the mountains, and a sleeping bag. Lee was very jumpy, but he agreed to let Carter take along his MAC 10 sub-machine gun and to hold off calling Hawk until later in the morning.

As soon as they had the camp located, Betty would be coming back to Bangkok where she would telephone Hawk and a strike force could be arranged.

"Watch yourself," Carter told Lee. "Call Colonel Trat in the morning and tell him that I left by military transport. If there's a leak in his office, which I suspect there might be, Kangting may believe for a little while that I've actually gone."

"It won't hold up for very long."

"I don't expect it will, but at least it'll give us a head start."

"How are you going to find the camp? There'll be plenty of security."

"We'll find it if it's there," Betty said. "The villagers will know." She'd brought along a thousand dollars in Thai money from the house, which was twice the annual income of many small villages.

"Good luck," Lee said.

"Thanks," Carter replied.

They had to drive the big Mercedes half off the road to

get around the still smoldering remains of the car whose gas tank Carter had hit with his shots. The gate had been left open. They drove through it and up onto the highway, then turned north, the night thick and dark. Except for a few patches of stars overhead, the sky was mostly overcast. They'd probably get rain before long, and perhaps snow by the time they reached the mountains.

Carter had not wanted to bring Betty along on this, but he felt he had no choice. His command of the language was adequate, but hers was perfect, and she knew the country far better than he did. And, as she had explained to him, villagers would often be more cooperative with an Oriental woman than they would be with an Occidental man.

They passed through Ayutthaya, a sleepy town about fifty miles north of Bangkok, at around two-thirty and pressed on north, rice fields stretching off in every direction as far as the eye could see. The first raindrops came a half hour later, and by three-thirty they were caught in a deluge and had to slow down to a crawl for about twenty miles.

The rain stopped gradually, as it had begun, and the sky began to clear to the north. Betty lay back in the seat and managed to get some sleep, though from time to time she would cry out, open her eyes, and look around. She looked up at Carter and smiled, then let her head roll back once again.

There wasn't much traffic on the highway during the night, only an occasional army truck or jeep. But by morning, as they approached Nakhon Sawan and, fifty miles beyond, the city of Phitsanulok, they began to pass a lot of people on foot, pulling carts loaded with farm produce for market.

They stopped for breakfast at a small inn just outside Phitsanulok, which would be the last decent-sized city they would encounter. From here on they would be following the Mae Nam River all the way up to the border with Laos, still nearly two hundred miles away.

Not many Western tourists came this far north, so restaurants catered mainly to Thais, for whom food wasn't really food unless it was laced with curry or *pri-kee-noo*, which were tiny red or green peppers that were extremely potent.

They each had a small bowl of *tom yam gung*, a delicious soup with greens and prawns, and a plate of *kao pat*, the Thai version of fried rice with crab meat, pork, chicken, onion, and egg, all of it washed down with a very good tea.

When they started out again, Carter felt much better, even though his mouth was on fire from the peppers.

"Not quite steak and eggs, is it," Betty said, laughing.

"It's a wonder half the country isn't writhing with stomach ulcers," Carter said.

"This food sticks to your ribs, Nick."

"Melts them too."

The land began to rise, the hills undulating in big waves north to the hazy horizon, the highway twisting and curving along the river. There were more trees the farther north they drove, and high in the hills they began to see and smell the pall of woodsmoke hanging over the land. It was from the charcoal kilns and fish-drying operations, Betty explained. Although here, with wood readily available, most people cooked and heated their homes with it as well. It smelled, Carter thought, a little like upstate New York in the fall, when everyone burned wood in their fireplaces.

As the land rose toward the mountains, the villages became smaller and farther between, the people along the road much poorer-looking. This close now to Laos, the Thais were still recovering from the effects of the fighting that had been going on for so long. A lot of Laotian refugees had crossed the border in the sixties and seventies and had not been able to get home again, nor would they ever. Laos was now closed to them.

They had stopped just before Phitsanulok for gas, and a hundred miles later they pulled over when Carter spotted a man selling gasoline from jerry cans stacked on a large wooden cart. He filled up the tank, and bought an extra can and gas for an exorbitant fee. He wasn't at all sure they would find more gas available where they were going.

By early afternoon they had made it all the way up into the mountains, some of the peaks ahead rising to ten thousand feet and more. These were the Tanen Taunggyi Range, down from which the Mekong River flowed. Not very far to the west, these mountains gave way to the mighty Himalayas, Mount Everest rising nearly thirty thousand feet above sea level. They were China's natural barrier against invasion from the south. Each pass through the mountains was closely guarded.

Higher and higher the road rose, and as it did it became narrower and narrower. The temperature began to drop as well. In the distance they could see the snow-covered peaks that Carter had crossed on his trek out of China. Looking at them now, he had to wonder how he had managed to come so far without proper food or clothing.

"You came over those?" Betty asked, as if she had read his mind.

"I don't know how," Carter said.

"I don't think Kangting knows who he's up against," she said. "If he did, he'd stop at nothing to kill you. It would be his first priority."

"Thanks for the vote of confidence. But we haven't got him yet."

"Somehow, looking at those mountains you crossed, I don't think he's got a chance in hell against you, Nick. I mean it."

Ban Pua was a substantial village of about ten or twelve thousand people barely twenty miles from the border with Laos. They reached it just before nightfall, parking the big car on the square behind the bus depot where an ancient, dilapidated GMC bus was parked. Carter knew they were attracting a lot of attention here, but he didn't think Kangting's people would put it together that fast, and he only intended on remaining here for a couple of hours at most before moving on.

They locked up and went across the street to the small inn. A dozen patrons were having drinks and an early supper at tables in an open courtyard, and Carter and Betty were given a table with a good view of the square by a young, exceedingly obsequious waiter.

"Welcome to our humble establishment," the young man said in barely understandable English.

"Our compliments to the owner," Carter said in passable Thai. "We would like two beers, please, and then some dinner."

"Ah, yes, of course. Very good," the boy said, and he scurried off.

"You got his attention," Betty commented when he was gone.

"And everyone else's attention as well," Carter said. Some children had gathered around their car, but an old woman came out of the bus depot and chased them away. She looked across the street at the inn, then turned and went back inside.

If Kangting was nearby, Carter figured, he would almost certainly have placed watchers in town to advise him of the appearance of strangers. Was the old woman one of them?

The inn's owner came out with two bottles of beer and glasses on a tray. He was dressed in a Western-style three-piece suit, sandals on his feet. He was slightly built, with thick dark hair and a thin mustache. When he smiled he displayed three gold-capped front teeth.

"Welcome, welcome," he said in English, pouring their beers. "You two lovely couple on vacation, please?"

"Honeymoon," Carter replied. "From Bangkok."

"Very good, honeymoon. Bangkok very far away."

"But we're also here on business as well," Carter said softly.

Betty leaned forward and opened her purse, taking out a thick wad of Thai currency. She covered it on the table with her hands. "I'm looking for my brother. He doesn't know yet of our wedding," she said in Thai.

"Yes? This is very interesting. This brother of yours, he lives here in Ban Pua?"

"We heard he might be nearby," Betty said. "In the mountains."

"He is a mountain man?" the owner said, laughing. "This is very funny. Maybe he is from Laos."

"Not Laos," Betty said. "Thailand. He is with friends. Many friends. They have a . . . camp in the mountains. A lot of money. Cars. Guns. Maybe even helicopters."

The owner was shaking his head. "Not here. Your brother is not here."

"But you don't know his name," Betty said, pushing the money a little closer.

"No, he could not be here. There is no camp like that around here. No, no. Perhaps you should return to Bangkok. That is a much better place for a honeymoon, much better. You should go back."

The little man was frightened; it was obvious. Carter knew that they had lucked out. Kangting was around here somewhere. And not very far. Not if Elizabeth had been able to drive to it in her Ferrari.

Betty started to push the money farther across the table, when Carter reached out and covered her hand with his. "Let's go, darling," he said in English. "I told you it would be useless. Let's just go back to Bangkok."

"Tonight?" she asked, playing along nicely.

"Why not? We can at least start back."

"Yes, I think that is good idea," the owner said in English.

"But first we would like some dinner," Carter said.

It was clear the man did not want to serve them, that he wanted them to leave immediately, but there wasn't much he could do without creating a scene. He personally took their order for a chicken dish and some rice, and probably broke a record for how fast he served them. All during their meal, which was quite tasty, he hovered around them, making sure everything was good, and that they were not dawdling. He wanted them out of his place as fast as possible.

By the time they had finished eating and paid their bill—the owner almost frantic in his effort to usher them out—it was dark and the courtyard was filled with patrons.

Carter and Betty both made a big show of telling the man how much they appreciated his help, and he almost fell over backward with fright.

"Help?" he squeaked. "What help? I have served you dinner, nothing more."

"Exactly," Carter said. "We understand."

"Thank you very much," Betty said loudly enough so that everyone in the courtyard heard her.

She took Carter's arm and together they left the restaurant, sauntered across the street, and got into the Mercedes. There were quite a few people in the square. Some boxes and crates were stacked up next to the bus, and the old woman from the depot stood in the doorway watching them.

Carter took his time starting the car and turning on the headlights. Betty was looking over his shoulder back toward the inn.

"Here comes someone," she said softly.

"Who is it?" Carter asked without turning.

"A young man. He was seated next to us with four other guys."

"What's he doing?"

"Watching us. . . . He's crossing the square."

Carter glanced over in time to see a young man dressed in dirty white slacks, a loose shirt, and sandals pass in front of the bus and stop at the coppersmith's booth. He took out a cigarette and lit it.

"I think it's time I bought a new copper pot for my

kitchen,'' Betty said, and she got out of the car.

Carter watched as she walked past the bus and stopped in front of the coppersmith's stall. She picked up a pot and looked at it. The young man glanced at her and said something. She nodded, and stepped around him to look at another pot, this one hanging from a hook. The young man said something else, and again Betty nodded. She took out some money from her purse and looked at it just long enough not to be too obvious. She said something, and the young man shook his head. He glanced across the street toward the inn, then said something else, and Betty handed him the money.

Carter put the Mercedes in gear and pulled away from the curb. He drove slowly past the bus, and as Betty stepped off the sidewalk, he stopped and reached across to open the door.

''Let's get the hell out of here,'' she said as she climbed in.

Even before she had her door closed he was moving down the street. Before he turned the corner he glanced up at the rearview mirror. Two men had come from the inn. The young man who had spoken with Betty took off in the opposite direction, the men sprinting after him.

''It's about fifteen miles from here, right up on the Laotian border,'' Betty said.

Carter headed back out of town to the highway that led north. No one was following them so far. ''Was he sure?''

''Sounded like it. Two weeks ago he saw Elizabeth's red Ferrari passing through town. There's been a lot of talk about a military unit up in the mountains. Men, big trucks, maybe even half-tracks. And the helicopters come in at night, he told me.''

''How does he know about this place?''

''He goes across the border into Laos two or three times a week. Cigarettes mostly. Sometimes medical supplies. He said he's known about the camp for nearly a year now.''

''Any mention of the Chinese?''

''He's never actually been to the camp. But he knew

approximately where it was from the helicopter traffic. He was afraid to get any closer. They all are. Kangting practically owns the town.''

They reached the open highway, and the road climbed farther up into the mountains, the night pitch-dark now as clouds rolled in. Kangting had picked the right spot. An entire army could he hidden here and never be spotted.

FOURTEEN

About three miles from the border with Laos, they almost missed the narrow dirt track that led to the west off the high mountain road. Running slowly without lights, the car's windows down, Carter thought he heard the sound of distant helicopters. He stopped the car.

The mountains were absolutely desolate. Nothing moved in any direction for as far as they could see. There was no traffic, no lights in any of the valleys and certainly on none of the distant peaks.

He opened the car door to get out and shut it immediately to turn off the interior lights. A light, chill wind blew down from the snow-covered fields, and he thought he heard the sound of rotors again, but then it was gone as quickly as it had come.

"What is it, Nick?" Betty asked softly from the car.

"Helicopters, I think. Toward the west. Three, maybe four of them, but a long ways off." He stepped away from the car and walked down the road to get away from the sound of its motor, when he spotted the dirt road leading back through the low scrub and rocks.

He motioned for Betty to remain where she was, and he stepped off the road and followed the track for about fifty yards. Suddenly it opened up and became a substantial un-paved road leading farther up into the mountains through the dense forests.

In the darkness, with only the starlight for illumination, he bent down and felt the ground. There were ruts. And the rocks and stones had been picked up and shoved around, as if a lot of traffic had come through here not so long ago. Heavy traffic. Big trucks. Perhaps even half-tracks.

He stood and listened a little longer, but the sounds of the helicopters were gone. Now he could hear only the whistle of the wind in the treetops. Nothing more.

Back at the car, he slipped behind the wheel.

"Where'd you go, Nick?" Betty asked.

Carter put the car in reverse and backed down the highway to the dirt track. "I found a road that leads back toward the west. There's been a lot of traffic recently."

"Kangting's camp?"

"I think it's a good possibility," Carter said. He glanced in the rearview mirror. Nothing moved on the road below toward Ban Pua, twenty miles away. He turned to Betty. "We'll follow the track for a while to make sure. But we're not going to get very close. He'll have sentries posted, I'm sure. But as soon as it looks as if this is it, you're going to drop me off and get back to Bangkok. Call Hawk. He'll know what to do. We'll have to get the Thai army and air force up here. Perhaps some of our boys as well."

She nodded grimly. Betty Chi Doi-ko was an excellent operative and wouldn't fold under pressure. Carter knew that he could count on her.

He glanced at his watch. It was still early. They had most of the night ahead of them. "With any luck you can be back in Bangkok by morning."

She nodded again, and Carter put the big Mercedes in gear and slowly nosed off on the road. For the first fifty yards the going was very rough. Several times the car bottomed out, the undercarriage scraping the rocks, but then the road smoothed out and they were able to make a little better time, though without lights he kept the speed down. To run off the road here would be a disaster.

The unpaved road wound its way through the forests, sometimes climbing up steep grades, sometimes plunging hundreds of feet down into narrow ravines. But always they headed northwest, paralleling the border with Laos, though at times he suspected they must have come within a few hundred yards of the actual frontier.

There were no signs of any human activity, other than the road, until at the base of a steep cut something at the side of the road caught Carter's eye and he pulled up.

Before he got out of the car, he reached up and took the lens off the dome light, and removed the bulb.

"What is it?" Betty asked.

"I don't know," Carter said. He got out of the car, crossed the dirt road, and at the edge of the road picked up an empty cigarette pack. Gauloises. The French cigarette. He'd noticed the white and blue pack because it stood out against the darker rocks.

He hurried back to the car and pulled open the door. "This is it," he said. "I found an empty cigarette pack, which meant someone was here. Possibly a sentry. I want you to get out of here now. You'll have to back up. There was a spot a half mile back where you should be able to turn around."

Betty jumped out and helped him gather the few supplies they'd brought along: food, sleeping bag, the MAC 10, boots and heavy jacket. They piled them alongside the dirt road, and Betty got in behind the wheel.

Carter reached in and kissed her on the lips. When they parted, she started to say something but he held her off.

"Later," he said. "Just get back to Bangkok and call Hawk."

"Good luck," she said.

"You too," Carter said, and he stepped back as she put the car in gear and slowly started backing up the way they had come.

He watched her leave, then he pulled off his shoes and put on the boots, then pulled on the jacket. Already the night was getting cold. By morning, he figured the temperature would probably be down around freezing or colder. In the winter these valleys would be impassable.

When the Mercedes was finally out of sight, Carter screwed the silencer on Whilhelmina, then shouldered the backpack with his food, sleeping bag, and the MAC 10, and headed up the road, moving carefully now in the night lest he stumble upon a sentry or trip some sort of detection device.

These mountains were wild and rugged. For the thousands of years of civilization in this part of the world, this area had not been settled, nor would it ever be. There probably were mountain huts where hunters might stay, but little else. Except for this carefully constructed road, and whatever lay at its end.

It was late when Carter thought he heard helicopters again, this time somewhere in the east. He figured he had gone at least ten miles from where Betty had dropped him off, and he was tired, his muscles burned, and it seemed as if he could never properly catch his breath. He found that he was stopping more and more often to rest at the side of the road. And he knew that he was becoming lax watching for sentries. The sounds of the chopper served to bring him around instantly, as if someone had splashed a bucket of cold water on his face.

He scrambled up from the side of the road into the protection of a thick stand of pine trees. The road here had dropped down from a flat low hill, and within twenty-five yards started back up toward a cut at least five hundred feet above where Carter stood.

The sounds of the helicopters were suddenly very close. Just to the south. Carter hunched down further in the protection of the overhanging branches as three choppers suddenly appeared over the hill from the south. Two of them were

U.S.-built Sikorsky HH-3E's, with huge payloads, while the third, much smaller machine, looked like a gunship to Carter. Though he couldn't immediately recognize the make, he had a strong suspicion it was Chinese.

The choppers flew straight across the valley, just topped the hill toward which the road rose, and then swung to the right as they dipped down.

Carter quickly stepped out from beneath the trees in time to see a single beam of light coming from the other side of the hill. It remained on for something under a minute and then went out.

A landing light to guide the helicopters in? If so, it meant the base was just on the other side, less than a mile off. This also meant security was either very lax or he had been very lucky getting this close.

His tiredness now all but forgotten, Carter made his way off the road, up over a tangle of boulders, and started up the hill on a path about twenty-five yards away from the clearing. The trees were very thick up the side of the steep hill, which provided not only cover, but the occasional hand-hold.

It took him nearly two hours to make it to the top, and he sagged back down against a big rock, his lungs aching, his breath coming in long, ragged gasps. The effects of the altitude and the ordeal of the past couple of weeks, combined with his lack of sleep and irregular meals since he had come back, were all catching up with him.

He took off his pack, sleeping bag, and the MAC 10, and laid them aside. The crest of the hill was about ten feet above him. When he caught his breath he crawled up through the trees, very careful to make absolutely no noise and to keep low.

At the top, he flattened himself against the ground and just peered up over the ridge. Below, about five hundred yards from his position, a large encampment was nestled in the trees at the base of a long, narrow valley. There were lights, but they were shielded from view from above; he was seeing just the sides of them. From the air the base would be completely camouflaged. Even as he watched, men were maneuvering the big choppers that had just come in beneath canopies that from above would look like the branches of trees. Carter estimated the base to be large enough to hold at least a thousand men in close quarters. From here he could smell woodsmoke mixed with the odors of spent helicopter fuel.

Another dirt track entered the camp from the opposite side of the valley. Carter figured they were less than a mile from the Laotian border. Under several other canopies he spotted troop transport trucks and at least four armored personnel carriers. Some of that equipment, he figured, had probably been airlifted from China to Laos and then brought up the back road to this camp.

The base reminded him of many of the CIA's training camps he had seen in Central America in recent years. From places such as this, elite forces were trained in secret to strike hard and fast. If Kangting's aim was a coup d'état of the Thai government, it looked as if he had the men and matériel to do it.

There seemed to be a lot of activity centered around the choppers that had just come in. More troops had come out of the barracks and were unloading crates of supplies from the two big machines. Weapons, he was certain, along with other supplies.

For the next hour he lay still, watching the unloading operation. When they were finished, the two big machines were again wheeled out to the open area at the center of the base. Their crews came out of the central building, climbed aboard, and moments later the choppers were started up and they lifted off, climbing out toward the east . . . toward Laos. And, Carter supposed, still another supply run.

Even from where he lay, Carter could easily see that there was a sense of urgency to the activities below, as if their zero hour was coming very soon—perhaps even sooner than they wished because of Kangting's trouble.

The supplies had been hastily carried to a spot to the west of the main building, where they had been stacked beneath another canopy. Carter was about to pull back when four people emerged from the building and walked around to the supplies. He recognized Kangting even from this distance. He was here! Any nagging doubts Carter might have had about Kangting's participation were now completely obliterated.

Whatever the man was really after, it involved the Chinese, who were supplying him arms through Laos, and it would involve force.

Kangting and the others went back into the main building, and for the moment at least, the base became quiet.

Carter had carefully scanned the perimeter of the base, looking for sentries or any sign that guards had been posted— a stray light from a cigarette, a movement, a noise, anything. But there was nothing out there, and it was bothersome to him that Kangting would not have been more careful. Was it arrogance, he wondered, or something else?

He pulled away from the crest of the hill and moved back down to where he had left his things. He found an overhanging boulder about twenty yards to the east, and he spread out the sleeping bag and ate a couple of the sandwiches they'd made back at the house. He drank a bottle of beer and then crawled into the bag to get a least a few hours of much-needed sleep. Betty would not be back in Bangkok to contact Hawk for at least another six hours. By the time something was set up with the Thai authorities and they could be airlifted up, it would be late in the afternoon, perhaps even dark. For the moment, there was little he could do except hang on, and keep low. As soon as the Thais showed up, he'd make his presence known.

From where he lay, he could just see a section of the dirt track he had followed, a narrow cut on the opposite hill to the south. He dropped off to sleep dreaming about Betty driving through the night, and hearing helicopters coming in every two hours.

• • •

Something woke Carter up. For a moment he lay still, every sense straining to hear or see what had disturbed his sleep. It was still dark, and now very cold. He looked at his watch. It was a little bit before four in the morning. He'd been asleep only a few hours, and his muscles were stiff from lying on the ground, but the edge of the weariness was gone, and he was completely alert.

He saw a flash of light from the dirt track on the hill to the south. It was a car. Someone was coming.

Carter climbed out of his sleeping bag and pulled on his jacket as he watched for the light again. He crawled out from beneath the overhanging rocks and hurried a few yards to the west. From there he could see down into the valley to where the road started up the hill.

A minute or so later he again saw the flash of headlights through the trees. They disappeared, then reappeared again, and the car came out into the open. It was the Mercedes! Betty's car!

From where he was he could not make out who was driving, but it was a safe bet it was not Betty. They'd taken her, evidently, and were bringing her back here. If indeed it was her now in the car, it meant there'd be no immediate help from the Thai army or air force. It would take Hawk a while before he would begin to believe that they were in trouble. And by then it could be too late, far too late.

He lost sight of the car again as it started through the trees up the hill, though from time to time he could see vague flashes of headlights through the branches.

Back at his supplies, he grabbed the MAC 10, checked its load, and stuffed the two extra clips of .45 ammunition into his pocket. He slung the compact submachine gun over his shoulder, pulled out Wilhelmina, made sure the silencer was screwed on tightly, and then scrambled back up to the crest of the hill. There he again flattened himself against the ground to watch what happened.

A minute later the Mercedes appeared on the road leading

down into the camp. As it passed about fifty yards out from the first building, a man stepped out of the trees, watched the car pass, then stepped back. They *had* posted sentries, but very close in. It was sloppy.

The Mercedes pulled up in front of the main building, and a man got out from the driver's side. A moment later the rear doors opened and two men in Thai army uniforms got out and pulled Betty from the car, screaming and kicking. Her hands were tied behind her back. She kicked at one of the men, who backhanded her, knocking her to the ground. Carter's grip tightened on Wilhelmina as they dragged Betty to her feet and hustled her into the building.

Carter waited a minute or two longer, deciding what he was going to have to do. Then he holstered his Luger, pulled out his stiletto, the blade gleaming in the starlight, and started down the side of the hill toward where he'd seen the lone sentry step out of the trees.

About halfway down the hill, Carter pulled up short as a husky man emerged from the main building, walked across the base to where the Chinese-built helicopter was parked, got something from inside, and came back.

It was the big guard, André. Carter recognized him by his bulk and by the way he walked. Before he went back inside, André turned and looked up toward the hill where Carter crouched behind a tree. He shook his head after a moment and went into the building.

Carter made it the remainder of the way down the hill in about twenty minutes, where he lay behind a jumble of rocks. A narrow clearing led from his position to a thick stand of trees, on the other side of which was the road. The sentry was barely twenty-five yards away now, but would be watching the road. He wouldn't be looking over his shoulder.

In the distance, over the hill, Carter could suddenly hear the sounds of the helicopters coming back, the deep chop of the rotors biting into the thin mountain air, echoing through the valley.

The Sikorskys appeared over the crest of the hill. A light came on at the edge of the landing area, and the big machines set down quickly. Several dozen uniformed men hurried out of one of the barracks a few hundrerd yards away. Two jeeps raced over to the helicopters, were hooked to the towing rings, and they expertly hauled the machines across to the canopies. Within fifteen minutes the machines were unloaded, dragged back to the clearing, and were airborne once again.

From his angle, Carter could see that the pile of supplies was huge; it was enough to supply an army of thousands of men. Whatever Kangting and his Chinese friends were planning was going to be very big.

Five minutes after the last sounds of the helicopters had died, Carter quickly crawled across the clearing and into the narrow stand of pine. He held up for another minute or so, then moved slowly forward.

Someone moved just ahead of him. Carter froze in his tracks. One of Kangting's guards from Bangkok—Carter recognized him from the compound—stepped around from behind a tree and leaned his rifle up against it. He sighed deeply, unzipped his trousers, and started to relieve himself.

Carter moved swiftly to the left so that he could come up on the man, keeping the tree between them.

The guard looked up in alarm at the last moment, but it was too late. Carter grabbed a handful of the man's uniform, hauled him backward against the tree, and slit his throat, blood rushing out of the gaping wound in a huge spurt. The man pitched forward, his last breath gurgling from his flooded lungs.

Turning on his heel, Carter quickly made his way through the line of trees to the edge of the first barracks. From inside he could hear a couple of men talking, but for the most part the camp was quiet. Most of the men, he figured, were sleeping. They would be roused only as the choppers came in with supplies.

He made his way behind four of the barracks, waiting a

minute at each corner and then racing to the next until he
had reached the canopy under which the latest batch of
supplies had been piled.

From the markings on the crates, most of the stuff was
Chinese: automatic weapons, including the Chinese version
of the BAR; grenade launchers; LAW rockets for use against
tanks and other armored vehicles; and at least a hundred
crates of hand-held ground-to-air missiles. These last were
American-made. Kangting had his sources.

Carter hurriedly opened one of the crates of American
Sparrow missiles and pulled out two. He had to duck down
as two soldiers came out of one of the barracks and crossed
over to the main building. The moment they were inside,
Carter hurried back the way he had come, stopping just
within the protection of the woods directly across from the
main building. From where he stood he had a clear shot at
the supply dump, the main building, and the approach that
the helicopters took coming in over the hill from the southeast.

He made two more trips back to the weapons cache, each
time bringing back with him four of the Chinese-made LAW
rockets, which were much smaller and more compact,
though no less deadly at close range, than the Sparrows.
Then he settled down to wait. If he and Betty were to get
out of here alive, they would need a diversion, and that was
what he was going to give them.

The eastern horizon was just beginning to grow light
when Carter heard the helicopters returning. He checked
both Sparrow missiles to make certain they were ready to
fire, and hefted one to his shoulder. He faced toward the
crest of the hill.

A diversion they needed, and a diversion they were going
to get.

FIFTEEN

Someone came out of the main building, and Carter had to step back out of sight. He looked over in time to see Kangting's big guard André stepping off the porch. The man stopped and looked thoughtfully up at the sky in the direction the helicopters were coming from. Then he glanced back toward the supply dump, and slowly let his gaze run around the perimeter of the camp.

André knew, or sensed, that something was wrong. He was good. The best. But there was no time now for a grudge match.

Carter hurriedly put down the Sparrow missile as the first chopper just topped the crest of the hill. He pulled out Wilhelmina and steadied his gun hand against the bole of a tree. It was a hundred-yard shot, but he'd made them before. And no one would hear the silenced shot.

André turned so that he was facing Carter, and he stiffened—had he seen something—just as Carter fired, the silenced shot lost in the noise of the rotors. André staggered backward, then sank to his knees and fell to the ground.

Carter holstered his Luger and snatched up the Sparrow, steadying it on his shoulder and sighting up through the rings at the lead helicopter, now barely two hundred yards away. He keyed the trigger. For a split second nothing happened, but then the missile took off with a tremendous burst of power.

For a moment Carter could see the missile in flight, but then it seemed to disappear. An instant later the big chopper exploded in midair, and then exploded once again as its cargo of ammunition caught.

Carter tossed the launching frame aside and grabbed the second missile as the other helicopter peeled right to avoid the falling wreckage. Oblivious of the sounds of men shouting, and a whistle blowing somewhere, Carter took careful aim and fired.

Even before the second missile had hit, Carter tossed down the launching frame. He snatched up one of the LAW rockets just as the chopper exploded, a tremendous *whump* that broke windows throughout the camp.

Men were streaming out of the barracks as Carter popped the tube, raised the LAW to his shoulder, and fired, the rocket running straight and true into the huge ammo dump.

This explosion was very large, completely knocking down a half-dozen barracks, and then bullets exploded, missiles took off, LAW rockets launched in every direction, killing some of the scattering troops outright, wounding others. It was as if an entire army had launched itself at the camp.

Carter tossed aside the spent LAW rocket tube, picked up another, and fired it along the row of barracks on the opposite side of the camp. The first one exploded in a big fireball that rolled over the others.

He fired a third and a fourth rocket, destroying other buildings in the camp, reducing the place to a burning pile of rubble.

There no longer was any discipline in the camp. What troops were still alive were heading away toward the thick forests that climbed the sides of the valley. They could not fight an enemy they could not see.

Carter looked over toward the main building in time to

see Kangting and four men in Chinese military uniforms racing toward the Chinese-made helicopter parked under the far canopy. He picked up another LAW rocket, popped the tube, and was about to bring it up to his shoulder when something very hard smashed into the small of his back, driving him forward onto his knees, the rocket clattering to the ground. Carter managed to roll over, a boot just missing his head.

It was André. He wasn't dead. Carter's shot had evidently just creased the man's head. A thin trickle of blood ran down the side of his face.

Carter scrambled back as André came after him. He yanked Wilhelmina from her holster and started to raise it, but André feinted left and kicked out, his boot catching Carter's gun hand. Wilhelmina flew off, bouncing against a rock.

André grabbed a handful of Carter's jacket, hauled him to his feet, and smashed him against a tree.

"I am happy that you came to me," the big man said. He smashed Carter against the bole of the tree again. "And now you will die!"

Carter kneed the man in the groin with all his strength, brought his two arms up, breaking André's grip, and then poked a left jab and a second into the man's face, driving him backward.

André was still with him, though. He bulled his way back, forcing Carter up against the tree again. This time André reached around Carter, grabbed the tree, and began to squeeze with all of his might, using his body to crush Carter against the tree.

Carter tried to struggle away, but André was just too big and too powerful to be pushed aside.

"You bastard," André hissed.

Carter put his arms around André as if he were hugging him. He was beginning to see stars, and he couldn't breathe, but he tensed the muscles in his right forearm and felt Hugo's haft in his palm. He nearly dropped it, but just before he started to black out, he buried the razor-sharp blade to the hilt in the big man's back.

For a long moment it seemed as if André hadn't even felt the knife, but then he stiffened and reared back with a bellow.

Carter shoved the man back, but André didn't go down. Carter hit him twice with left jabs, putting everything he had into it, the big man's head snapping back, and then he smashed a roundhouse right into the man's face, splitting his nose. And still André didn't go down. The man was incredible. He was a machine, not a human being.

Carter was conscious of the sounds of the Chinese-built helicopter starting up. He had to end this now, before Kangting escaped. He shoved André back, and hit him again with a right hook. Then again, and again. Each time, the huge guard's head snapped back and he was stunned, but he refused to give up.

It was no longer neat or clean. With each blow, a little more of André's face was destroyed. Blood streamed in his eyes, from his mouth and broken jaw, and from his split nose.

Slowly the big man began to sag to his knees, and still Carter smashed blow after blow into his face.

At the end, Carter brought his fists together and smashed them with every ounce of his remaining strength into the base of André's skull, the man's neck snapping with a loud pop.

Carter staggered backward. This was one kill he would never forget. One that he would never be proud of.

He turned in time to see the helicopter bearing Kangting and his Chinese allies just lifting off. Quickly he snatched up a LAW rocket, extended the tube, raised it to his shoulder, and led the rising helicopter. He pressed the firing stud, and a second later the helicopter exploded in a huge ball of flames, burning debris raining down over the camp.

Tossing the spent launching tube aside, Carter grabbed his MAC 10 and raced out of the woods and across the clearing toward the main building, which was now burning furiously. Someone moved to his left, and without breaking stride he snapped off a quick burst, killing the man.

Two other soldiers came around the corner of the building, and Carter shot them from the hip, the MAC 10's .45-caliber bullets smashing into their chests, driving them backward.

He kicked open the door and leaped inside the building. Smoke was everywhere, and down a long corridor he could see that the entire back of the building was in flames.

"Betty!" he shouted, leaping over a desk and starting down the corridor.

"Nick?" she cried. She was somewhere in the back.

Carter raced down the corridor, smashing open doors as he went. "Betty! Where are you?"

"Here! Nick, here!"

The room she was in was already on fire. She was hand-cuffed to a steel chair. He pulled her aside, her arm extended, and fired a short burst that broke the handcuff's chain.

She collapsed in his arms then, and he had to half drag, half carry her back up the corridor, the ceiling caving in just behind them.

The camp was completely on fire now, the flames rising hundreds of feet up into the morning sky, a thick black pall of smoke drifting upward to be caught in the mountain breezes.

A pair of F-15s with U.S. Air Force markings suddenly swooped in low over the hills from the south and made a pass over the camp, climbing out at the end of the valley and coming around again.

"You didn't contact Bangkok?" Carter asked Betty.

"No, I didn't, Nick. They caught up with me about seventy-five miles south of here. It was a military roadblock."

Carter looked up as the jets came around again, and he waved. "It was Hawk," he said. "Lee must have called him from your office, and Hawk ordered the strike."

They could hear the sounds of helicopters now, a lot of them, and from over the hill a troop truck appeared on the dirt track, and then another, and another, and even more.

It was over, finally. Kangting had lost. The Chinese government had lost. And the Thais had won.

Carter and Betty stumbled down to the road to meet the convoy. "Did you see Elizabeth Kangting here?" he asked.

Betty looked up and shook her head. "No. Did you?"

"She might have been in Kangting's helicopter," Carter said, looking over at the smoldering debris. "If she was here, she's dead now."

The operation was a joint Thai-U.S. effort, arranged, the commander who was a Thai army colonel said, through "friends" in Washington.

"It appears that you are a lucky man, Commander Carson," the colonel said. "And you, Miss Doi-ko, are the most tenacious newspaperwoman I have ever met."

Despite their injuries, despite their weariness, and despite the fact that they'd almost been killed several times in the past few days, Carter and Betty began to laugh, unable to help themselves. Tears ran down their cheeks, and their sides ached, and still they laughed. The colonel shook his head, ordered the medics to check them out, and left to supervise the mopping-up operation. They continued to laugh, in relief as much as for anything else. Because now it was truly over, and they both understood that they were going to have some time together. In peace.

It was well after noon by the time the remainder of Kangting's troops had been rounded up. Not one of the fifty Chinese regular army soldiers had surrendered. One by one they had to be hunted down and killed. It was just as well, the Thai colonel said. They could never had been returned to China because the Chinese government would never have admitted they were here in the first place. Nor could they have remained, because the Thai government would not have admitted they were here either.

Carter and Betty were taken by chopper to the American

Hospital in Bangkok, arriving at around five that afternoon. After the doctors had looked them over—except for some cuts and bruises, and extreme fatigue, they both were in remarkably good condition considering their ordeal—Colonel Trat came in and congratulated them.

"Though exactly for what, I don't quite know," he said. "But my government is happy, and so am I, though it may be some while before my city is back to normal. Mr. Kangting's loss will be deeply felt. A most unfortunate air accident, you know."

"Yes," Carter said. "I know."

Thomas Lee picked them up at seven, bringing them over to the AXE office where Betty hurriedly made out a brief report as Carter telephoned Hawk, telling his boss all that had happened, and thanking him for calling out help.

"I figured it would only be a matter of time before you actually found the camp and starting raising hell," Hawk said. "I told our pilots to look for a lot of smoke. You'd be sure to be close."

"So what was he after, sir? Did we ever figure it out?" Carter asked.

"It was everything you'd thought, Nick. Kangting, with help from the Chinese, was planning a coup d'état. The Chinese, in return for trade agreements, were going to give the administration of Hong Kong to Kangting in 1997, if he was still alive and able to take the job."

"On top of it all the Chinese were double-crossing him?" Carter asked.

"In a way. They figured a man of Kangting's stature couldn't possibly fail, so they set him up, unwittingly, as bait to lure you or someone like you into their trap. They wanted to see what they could come up with as an added bonus."

"And it very nearly worked," Carter said.

"Yes, it did, Nick," Hawk said. "Now, I don't want to see you back here in the office for . . . let's say a week?"

"Ten days, sir?"

"Ten days it is. And give my regards to Miss Doi-ko."

Lee had gotten them another car, and by ten they were pulling up in front of Betty's brother-in-law's house outside the city. The AXE people had done a good job cleaning up the mess, including the burned-out car on the driveway.

Inside they held each other close for a long time, and then they kissed. When they parted, Betty was a little breathless.

"Now I'll take that cognac, Commander Carson. You may pour if you wish. I'll run our bath."

"We've got ten days."

"I know," she said. "Let's not waste any of them."

She turned and walked into the bedroom, shedding her clothes as she went.

The tapes were still in the machine. Carter rewound them and turned the music on low. He found another bottle of cognac and a couple of glasses. He poured himself some, sipped it, and then pulled off his jacket and his weapons, laying them on the coffee table. This time he wasn't bringing Wilhelmina with him. This time there was no need. Because it was over.

Slipping out of his shoes, he picked up the bottle and glasses and went into the bedroom. The lights were very low, and a soft, warm breeze came from the back through the open sliding glass doors. Betty had not yet started to run the bathwater, but he could see the rest of her clothing in a heap on the floor—her skirt and blouse, her sandals, and her bra and panties.

"Betty?" he said softly, coming into the bedroom.

"Isn't this sweet?" Elizabeth Kangting said from the shadows.

Carter spun around. Betty, nude, her hands raised over her head, stood up against the wall. Elizabeth stood a few feet away from her, a big military .45 automatic in her little fist. She was dressed in an evening gown, gold slippers on her feet, her hair done up at the back, a diamond tiara above her forehead. Her face was pale, her eyes were red-rimmed, her lips white.

"We thought you were dead," Carter said.

"Sorry to disappoint you, Nicholas."

"Your father and the others are dead. It's all over now, Elizabeth."

"Not quite," she said. "One last bit of unfinished business."

"Why?" Betty asked. "What can you hope to gain by—"

"Quiet," Elizabeth hissed as she turned the gun toward Betty.

At that moment Carter threw the bottle of cognac at Elizabeth. She reflexively ducked, the .45 going off, the noise loud in the confines of the room, the bullet smacking into the wall across the room.

Betty was on her in the next instant, pushing her gun hand aside and smashing her back against the wall.

The gun went off again, this time the bullet exploding a table lamp inches from where Carter stood. The women went down on the tile floor, crying and biting and screaming as they rolled over and over. Elizabeth was fighting like a madwoman, and though Betty was well trained and strong, she was having trouble controlling the situation.

Carter stepped across to them just as Elizabeth's gun hand came free and she started to bring the .45 around toward Betty. He grabbed the gun out of her hand and stepped back.

"It's over!" he shouted. "Enough!"

With a gigantic heave, Elizabeth shoved Betty aside and scrambled nimbly to her feet. Her eyes were wild. A little blood dribbled down from her nose, and she'd lost her tiara. She fumbled in the folds of her dress, and suddenly she had a sheathed knife in her hands. She yanked out a long, gleaming blade, tossing the sheath aside.

"Don't!" Carter shouted, raising the .45.

Betty was still on the floor, looking up at Elizabeth. "Don't do it, Miss Kangting," she said.

Elizabeth was looking at them, a little spittle dribbling from the corner of her mouth, her breasts rising and falling with her rapid breathing.

"You will go to jail," Carter said, "but with your father's fortune it won't last very long. You'll be out and free."

"You bastard!" she screeched. "I let you make love to me, and in return you killed my father!"

"Put the knife down—" Betty started to say, but Elizabeth suddenly grabbed the haft with both hands, turning the blade inward, and she drove it to the hilt into her own chest, just below her left breast, a great geyser of blood spurting out.

"Oh," she cried softly, and then her body went slack and she fell on the floor, dead.

Their ten days together passed as if in a dream. They flew to Hong Kong—Bangkok had too many bad memories for them—where they spent their days seeing the sights, their nights out dining and dancing, and the cool of the morning they made love in their palatial suite at the Regal Meridien.

All of it was on Carter's AXE expense account, but somehow this time he didn't think Accounting was going to give him too much static. This time he and Betty had earned it.

They went to the horse races, betting outrageously and losing just as badly, though Betty did pick one long shot for a big bundle. They took the harbor cruise, visited Macao, and on their eighth day had dinner at the U.S. consulate.

"So, what happens next?" Betty asked on their last day together as Carter was getting ready to fly out.

"We return to work. Me in Washington, you in Bangkok."

"I meant about us?"

The question had been coming all along, and Carter had done a lot of hard thinking. "I don't want to become another Tommy Bruce for you."

She nodded her understanding, though it didn't make her happy. "You're right, of course. I don't think I could take it if anything happened to you."

"Neither could I, if something happened to you. We'd be vulnerable."

"So I marry a banker and have a slew of kids and live happily ever after?"

"Something like that."

She smiled. "Once they've seen Paree, you can't expect them to go back to the farm." She shook her head. "But we'll see each other again, won't we?"

Carter took her in his arms and they kissed deeply. "Count on it," he said. "You can count on it."

DON'T MISS THE NEXT NEW
NICK CARTER SPY THRILLER

BLOODTRAIL TO MECCA

Constance Graves rose from the bubbles in the large, sunken tub. She flipped open the tub's stopper, stepped into the nearby shower stall, and revolved the spigots. The nozzle above her head gushed as the swishing sound of the water from the tub gurgled through the escape trap.

She shampooed her hair thoroughly and then rinsed it. At the same time, she thought of Nick Carter. The image of his tall, muscular body floated before her eyes as the warm water cascaded over her bare breasts. The image made her smile.

She decided she wouldn't dress for dinner right away. When he returned she would be waiting for him, still nude . . . on the bed.

Her hands were just reaching for the shower knobs when the glass door of the shower opened with a crash.

She saw two things at once: a black image, and a knife

coming at her. She threw herself to the side and the blade bit into her shoulder.

The slash brought a scream of pain to her lips. More from irrational fear than calculated intent, she lunged forward. Constance Graves was a big woman, inches taller than her attacker.

Her surprise move caught Ian Slade unawares. Her shoulder slammed him full in the face, sending him sprawling through the bathroom door to the floor of the hall.

As she jumped over him, Slade slashed again, the blade leaving a gushing red line on her left buttock.

This brought another howl from the woman as she leaped over the bed toward the phone.

Slade went after her. The hand holding the phone was just coming up when Slade chopped her wrist. There was a crack as the bone broke, and then he was wrestling her to her back. He mashed his left hand over her face and lifted the knife in his right.

Through his splayed fingers, Connie saw the knife descending. She tried to scream but there was no sound.

Then there was nothing but blackness.

Bloodlust surged through Slade's body. Again and again the knife descended. Finally the fact that she was dead penetrated.

Ian Slade rolled from the body, gasping for air.

The bitch had been as strong as a man.

He looked down at his black turtleneck and trousers. They were covered with blood. It would be hell if he were spotted now.

Quickly, he snapped off the light in the bedroom and moved into the sitting room.

He was just snapping off that light when he heard the key in the door.

Carter opened the door. He was half inside before his built-in warning system went off.

It was too late.

A dark figure hurtled out of the darkness against the door, cutting off all light. Carter dived for the floor just in time to avoid a killing blow. As it was, the knife bit into his thigh.

Carter hit the parquet and immediately whiplashed his body. He caught his attacker at the knees, sending him in a dive down the three steps into the sunken living room.

Instantly the Killmaster was on his feet, groping for the light switch. He hit it and saw the short, wiry man wildly reaching for the knife he had dropped.

They both saw it at once, and dived. Only the little man changed direction. He came up on his knees and grabbed a lamp from the table beside the sofa.

As Carter came down, Slade whirled, slamming the heavy base into Carter's face. A million red lights went off and he was looking up at a foot coming at him through blood.

He managed to get his hands up in time to grasp the other man's ankle. He twisted, and the momentum sent the black-clad figure crashing into the bar. Glasses and bottles scattered everywhere, and a wall mirror shattered on the floor with a crash that would wake the dead.

Carter struggled to his feet, still groggy, wiping the blood from his eyes. He could feel that his left trouser leg was soaked, also with his own blood.

The other man was on his knees now, his arms at his back. Carter took a step forward, and the hands came forward. In them was a short-barreled revolver.

Carter ducked and spun to his left, his right leg kicking.

His foot struck the gun hand as his spin caught the other man off-balance. The explosion was like a cannon going off in the room.

The slug hit the huge pane of one of the French doors leading to the terrace, and the glass exploded.

Carter threw a chop to the man's jaw, but Slade stepped back, avoiding the blow.

Then the blood cleared enough from the Killmaster's eyes

so that he could make out the killer's features.

Ian Slade. Carter knew him from a hundred photographs he had seen in years past.

Just the man's identity told him that he would have to kill him quickly or be killed himself.

Carter grabbed for the gun and managed to get Slade's wrist. The killer almost wrenched himself free, but Carter wrapped his arm around Slade's so that he held the gun hand in a hammerlock.

They struggled, Carter's back against the smaller man's chest. Then Slade smashed the heel of his free hand into Carter's face, and kept smashing.

The bastard is little, Carter thought, *but he's strong and faster than hell*. Also, he had lost a lot of blood, and was still losing.

Slowly he was losing his grip on Slade's gun hand. At the same time, he realized that the little man was maneuvering him toward the French doors and the balcony.

Carter tried to exert force in the opposite direction, but his strength had ebbed until they were about equal.

Slade maneuvered him closer and closer. Suddenly Carter lunged forward, pulling Slade off-balance. He thrust the man's hand through the shattered pane and raked it from side to side over the jagged glass.

Slade, startled, bellowed in pain. As he tried to yank his arm free, Carter put all his weight on it, slashing the arm from elbow to wrist.

Again Slade screamed, this time as much from the fountain of his own blood spewing as from the pain. His fingers opened and the gun fell to the deck of the balcony.

"Now, you little son of a bitch," Carter growled.

He grabbed Slade by the hair and threw him across the room. He went sprawling over the couch, knocked over a chair and table, and somehow ended up on his feet against the far wall.

In amazement, he held up his mutilated arm and gazed at the ripped flesh that hung in blood-dripping tatters.

He looked at Carter, then at the arm, and then back to Carter.

Like a cornered cat, his eyes blazed at the source of his pain. With a squealing scream, he charged his enemy. Again Carter tried to evade, but the man was too fast.

He hit the Killmaster in the chest, and both of them tumbled onto the balcony. The smaller man sat on Carter's chest, his knees pinning the AXE man's arms and hands like the bite of a ferret around the throat.

Carter tried to buck him off, but he couldn't as he felt the thumb-pressure on his windpipe increase. He gasped for air and none would come. Drums started pounding in his ears as he rolled his head from side to side.

Then he spotted the revolver. He managed to get one arm free, and crawled his fingers across the thin, slick carpeting.

"Bastard, fucking bastard!" Slade was growling, the blood pumping in gushes from his shattered arm.

Then Carter's fingers found the cold steel. He stuck the barrel as far as he could into Slade's gut and pulled the trigger twice.

The sound was muffled, but the vibration from the blast slithered through the man's arms down to Carter's throat.

Then the hands were gone.

—From BLOODTRAIL TO MECCA
A New Nick Carter Spy Thriller
From Jove in March 1988